PHILIPPA DOWDING

We acknowledge financial support for our publishing activities: the Government
of Canada through the Canada Book Fund and The Canada Council for the Arts;
the Government of Ontario, through the Ontario Arts Council, Ontario Creates,
and the Ontario Book Publishing Tax Credit. We acknowledge additional funding
provided by the Government of Ontario and the Ontario Arts Council
to address the adverse effects of the novel coronavirus pandemic.

LIBRARY AND ARCHIVES CANADA CATALOGUING IN PUBLICATION

Title: Firefly / Philippa Dowding.
Names: Dowding, Philippa, 1963– author.
Identifiers: Canadiana (print) 20200340727 | Canadiana (ebook) 20200340743 |
ISBN 9781770865983 (softcover) | ISBN 9781770865990 (HTML)
Classification: LCC PS8607.O9874 F57 2021 | DDC jC813/.6—dc23

United States Library of Congress Control Number: 2020950452

Cover art: Julie McLaughlin
Interior text design: www.tannicegdesigns.ca

Printed and bound in Canada.
Manufactured by Houghton Boston in Saskatoon, Saskatchewan,
Canada in September 2021.

DCB
AN IMPRINT OF CORMORANT BOOKS INC.
260 Spadina Avenue, Suite 502, Toronto, ON M5T 2E4
www.dcbyoungreaders.com
www.cormorantbooks.com

For Doane

ONE

The Corseted Lady

"What'll it be, Fifi?"

"It's *Firefly*." I say this slowly.

"*Formerly* Fifi," I add, to be kind.

There are pancakes on the stove. Real pancakes. Aunt Gayle waves the spatula in the air.

Spatula. Weird word.

"Sorry. What'll it be, *Firefly*? Syrup or jam on your pancakes?" Aunt Gayle dumps a plate of pancakes in front of me, and my mouth waters. Hard. I clamp my lips shut.

I am not a dog.

But really, when was the last time I had pancakes?

"Can I have both?" Aunt Gayle opens the fridge door and pulls out two bottles, maple syrup and strawberry jam, and plunks them on the table in front of me.

I swallow. I pour syrup and spoon out jam. I hope she doesn't notice my hand shaking.

I eat.

Aunt Gayle sits across the table, lights a cigarette, takes a deep drag. Watches me, squinting through the smoke.

I slow down. Close my eyes. Chew.

Food.

I open my eyes. A last ray of October early-evening light pierces through the kitchen window and lands on my plate of pancakes. It lights my hands, falls across my face. Like a sign. Aunt Gayle takes another long drag of her cigarette and looks at me.

I chew. I swallow. I don't eat like a dog, although I could.

"Hungry, huh?" she says in a careful way. I shrug, nod, notice a full glass of orange juice in front of me, and drain it in one long chug. I draw the back of my hand across my mouth.

ORANGE JUICE. I can't remember the last time I had all I wanted of that, either. The case workers and thera-pists at the Jennie Smillie Robertson Women's Center (but everyone just calls it Jennie's) kept the orange juice locked in the fridge, along with the methadone.

I reach for the carton and pour another glass.

This one, I sip.

I can't possibly answer her question. Hungry? That's not really the word. Empty. Diminished. Shriveled.

Distorted. I finally settle on Dangerous. I'm *dangerous* with hunger. Aunt Gayle sits patiently, her cigarette burning slowly, smoke unwavering, straight up to the ceiling. That's how still she sits.

No questions yet. I guess that'll come.

I finish my plate of pancakes and try not to belch. Something reminds me that it isn't particularly polite to belch after you eat, although no one has told me that for a while. When it's clear I've finished, my aunt stubs out her cigarette, leaves the kitchen, and heads out into the darkness of the shop.

I hear industrial lights buzz to life in the shop ceiling.

"Come on, I'll show you your room. It's upstairs in the apartment," she says. "Do you want me to carry that?" she asks, pointing to the garbage bag of clean clothes at my feet, courtesy of Jennie's. I grab it, clutch it to me.

"No, that's okay," I say. It's *my* garbage bag full of clean clothes, thank you Aunt Gayle. I follow my aunt out of the kitchen.

We step into The Corseted Lady.

It's one of Canada's oldest film costume shops, but it's a warehouse. Not a little shop. It has two stories of costumes, floor to ceiling. The stupid social worker kept babbling on about it in the car on the way over: seven million pieces, established in 1984, costumers to the stars.

It is impressive, though. I shuffle after my aunt, and take quick looks at the costumes in racks, all around me.

Bright orange, handmade signs hang at the end of every rack.

We swing past the first row of costumes.

Police Uniforms, 20th Century.

Motorcycle Cop Boots, Sizes 8-12.

19th Century Smoking Jackets.

Victorian Era, Girl's Clothes.

Women's Bloomers, 1920.

Clowns & Harlequins, 18th Century Players.

Dickens Era, Flower Girls & Street Urchins, 1880s.

I look away.

Aunt Gayle leads me up a set of old wooden stairs to the second floor.

"Is this ... is this where you live?" It's kind of weird to say goodbye to the kitchen, then walk through racks and racks of clothes to head upstairs to an apartment. What is this place?

Aunt Gayle nods. "I know, it's a little strange until you get used to it. The whole building is the costume shop. The kitchen is downstairs but the apartment is up here on the second floor. It was once a horse stables and carriage turnaround, so it's a bit eccentric."

At the top of the stairs, I have to stop.

The second floor is just wall-to-wall costumes.

"Do you remember this place, Firefly?" she asks as she leads me through the racks of costumes. Seven million pieces really is a lot. Costumes vanish in the distance, all the way to the windows on the far wall of the warehouse.

"Not really. Well, barely." I'm really not sure if I do or I don't.

Wedding Dresses, 1930s.

Wedding Dresses, 1940s.

Party Dresses, (Cocktail & Formal), 1950s.

"The apartment is back here." We stop at a heavy, old, wooden door, and Aunt Gayle pushes it open. More lights buzz on.

And we step into a large, bright apartment. The walls are brick, and Aunt Gayle has art, very interesting art, hanging all over. At the far end is a living room with a gas fireplace, chunky chairs, and floor-to-ceiling windows looking over the neighborhood. Closer, there's a bathroom and three shut doors in a narrow hall.

"Here's your room," Aunt Gayle says, pushing open the first door. "It's the guest room. Or … it was." She looks at me, awkward for a moment.

"Hot bath sound good?" she adds, brightening, and disappears down the hall.

I nod. A *hot* bath? Jennie's had showers, but they were cold. I add the word to the growing list of "Things I've Almost Forgotten."

Pancakes. Hot bath.

I stand alone in what is to be my bedroom.

There's a bed. A chest of drawers. A closet. A small window over a tiny desk with a chair. I snap the reading light on, then off. I peer out the window for a second, get a glimpse of the neighborhood: trees, roofs, backyards, laneway. In the middle distance toward the setting sun, the pointy CN Tower.

Good to know the lay of the land, as Joanne-the-mother always said. No, *says*, I guess. She's still alive.

It's just a normal room. Light blue.

There's a mirror. Over the chest of drawers.

I peek at myself, really fast.

Look away.

I hear my aunt turning on the faucets in the bathroom down the hall. She hums quietly, bustling around. Hot water is filling the deep, old-fashioned tub.

I clutch my garbage bag of clothes. I can't sit anywhere. It's all too clean.

I stretch out on the bench, pull my AC/DC hoodie over my face. I peek across the park. The lights are on at Joanne-the-mother's house: the upstairs hall light, the light in the front room. My bedroom window is dark, though. I check Moss Cart's watch: 1:45 a.m. Joanne-the-mother lurches past the downstairs window. Still awake.

A spectacular CRASH comes from inside the house ...

A tap on the door. "Your bath's ready, Firefly."

I stand, blinking. It takes a minute. Who's that? Bath? Oh yeah.

That's Aunt Gayle. I'm in the apartment on the second floor of The Corseted Lady costume shop, with seven million costumes in the warehouse around me. There's a bed. A bathroom.

I know where I am. I'm in my aunt's costume shop.

But ... what exactly am I doing here?

TWO

Rolling Judy

Soap.

I hold a light purple bar in my hand. It's brand new, the logo is still sharp. Aunt Gayle must have opened it just for me.

I sink into hot water. The tub is huge. There's a parrot statue looking down at me from the tiny window high up the wall, a bare tree branch tosses against the evening sky outside.

A gentle tap at the door, and I'm alert. I locked the door when I shut it. I'm not going to give up the chance to use a lock, now am I?

"Um, Firefly? Should I wash your clothes on the floor out here?" Aunt Gayle says through the door. There's an outer door to the bathroom, where the sink is, and an inner door for the toilet and tub. I guess that kind of works, for privacy anyway.

I left the clothes I was wearing out by the sink. The garbage bag of clean clothes is still in the bedroom.

"Maybe?" I answer. I don't really want her to touch my clothes, to be honest. But then ... they have to get washed some time.

Fine, Aunt Gayle. Wash them.

I hear her stoop and pick up my clothes. Then she lets out a soft *gasp*. Yeah. They're pretty filthy. I mean, Joanne-the-mother wasn't exactly big on taking us to do the laundry.

"Firefly? Honey? Would ... well, would it be better if I just ... toss them?"

I'm silent. They're my clothes, Aunt Gayle. Do you mind? I picked through a lot of Jennie's clothing boxes to find them. They're mine. I want to keep them. Especially my AC/DC hoodie. She reads my silence through the door, somehow.

"You know, sorry. That was stupid. It's okay. I'll put them in the big washer. I'll wash all your other stuff, too? Is that okay? The stuff in the garbage bag? The stuff you brought?"

Jennie's clean might not be your clean. Better wash it all, Aunt Gayle.

"Yes." I'm having a hard time getting words out properly.

"There's a bathrobe and towel in there, in the closet beside the toilet. I'll leave some more of Amanda's clothes in your room while I wash yours. Okay?"

"Yes. Thank you." Is that my voice? I sound like a robot. Amanda. Nice, older cousin Amanda. Amanda who is now at law school in Kingston, Aunt Gayle says. Do I remember her? Maybe? Vaguely? Sort of?

I hear Aunt Gayle move away from the door.

Then I roll around in the soapy, lavender-scented water for a long, long time. I keep draining water when it gets cooler, then add more hot.

Hot water. A miracle.

I try for a while to remember the last time I was here. At The Corseted Lady. The last time Joanne-the-mother dragged me along to visit her older sister, Aunt Gayle.

I must have been pretty little. I was in junior school — so seven or eight maybe — the last time we visited. So six years ago at least.

I hold the lavender soap, send a soapy wave of water to my toes. Then I do suddenly have a memory.

Cousin Amanda laughing. We push two of those weird, headless mannequin things on wheels. We race them up and down between the racks.

Rolling … Bettys? Rolling Susies?

No. Rolling *Judys*. The weird, headless mannequins are called Rolling Judys. And Amanda and I pushed them up and down the hall together, laughing our butts off.

I spend a long time washing my hair.

It's not too long — just past shoulder length — since

they gave free haircuts at Jennie's every other Wednesday. But dirty?

Oh yes.

I carefully wash every part of my body. I wash my hair twice until it squeaks when I run a hand down a strand. I spend a lot of time between my toes since I can finally see them.

My fingernails, too. Wow. Caked in dirt, from ... some of it is probably from the summer.

I wash my neck, my back, behind my knees. The lavender soap gets a good workout; it's smaller by the time I'm finished, the brand name less clear.

I finally leave the bath. Pull the plug, watch the water drain away.

And NO! The ring around the tub is ... I can't even describe it.

I panic. I *cannot* leave that ring for Aunt Gayle!

I dig under the sink and find some tub cleaner and a clean sponge. I snap on the yellow rubber gloves and crouch in the tub. I scrub.

It takes a while. The ring of filth is as wide as my hand, and it left smaller rings as the tub drained. I clean away, swearing. The director at Jennie's didn't like it much, but when I cleaned their kitchen, I'd swear as hard as I could. It gives me focus, I'd tell her. She'd smile, hand me a plastic-wrapped turkey sandwich, two cookies, and a ten-dollar bill for the hour of work.

A few minutes later, the tub is clean. Cleaner. Clean, though, is entirely relative, after a while.

I find a thick, gray bathrobe in the closet and pad back to the bedroom. No sign of Aunt Gayle. A small pile of clothes is neatly folded on the bed.

I pick up a pair of Amanda's old pajamas. *The Little Mermaid*? I sigh. I pick through some more of the pile and find a pair of blue track pants with "Queen's" on them, but a good rip in the knee, and a clean but suitably worn out *My Little Pony* T-shirt. I pull on some thick, brown wool socks. They look and feel handmade.

Does Aunt Gayle knit socks, I wonder?

The importance of clean, dry socks is seriously underrated.

These will do. I get a stab looking at the T-shirt, though.

Moss Cart would love it. His shopping cart is covered in *My Little Pony* figures, tied in place like tiny, plastic prisoners. He lives in the park with his unholy army of shiny, sparkly creatures, protecting all his carefully collected things.

Moss Cart sits beside me on the park bench, and rips the sub sandwich in half. I take a bite of cucumber, cheese, rosemary bread and my stomach lurches and groans. Food. So good. He hands me a lukewarm coffee and we sit and watch the sun go down across the park. My house is quiet, dark. Joanne-the-mother must be out somewhere. Can't imagine where. Or passed out. Or sitting in the dark with the lights turned out, which she does a lot. A group of high school kids walk past. Moss Cart nudges me.

"Your crew?" he asks and I shake my head.

"I have no crew. You're my crew, Moss Cart …"

I wear the *My Little Pony* T-shirt and descend the old wooden stairs to the kitchen on the main floor.

Aunt Gayle is knitting at the kitchen table, a cigarette burning in the ashtray beside her. She looks up and smiles. She puts her knitting down and goes to the stove. She stirs something in a pot, then pours the contents into a mug and places it on the table in front of me.

"A little hot chocolate before bed?"

I nod and wrap my arms around myself. I consider asking her for a cigarette, but the truth is, although Joanne-the-mother smokes and I do too sometimes, I don't really like it.

"Hungry?" she asks. "I can make anything. Pizza? Chili? A teriyaki-chicken salad?"

My stomach growls, but I just ate a huge plate of pancakes an hour ago. I better pace myself here. No puking on the first day.

"No thanks. I'm still kind of full from the pancakes." Aunt Gayle takes a long look at me.

"Do you want me to braid your hair?" she asks.

The thought of having my hair braided is so odd, so foreign, that I must look like I'm considering it. The next moment, she pushes me into a seat and pulls out a long comb and two hair bands from a drawer.

I sit quietly perched on the edge of the chair in the kitchen as my aunt expertly, and gently, splits my hair in a severe part, right down the middle. Then she works it into two cool braids.

We don't talk, but it's okay. She has some music on her laptop on the counter. I don't recognize it, but music hasn't been a big part of my life lately. It sounds like country music.

A cat face appears at the door. It stares up at me for a second, then slowly, slowly, reveals itself: a huge, ugly, orange tomcat with a torn ear and a ragged nose, and way too many toes on one paw. Cat-face stares at me a moment longer then slinks to cat food dishes on a mat beside the fridge. Cat-face commences nibbling of cat crunchies.

Aunt Gayle braids away.

"That's Juggers, short for Juggernaut. He's a stray, not terribly pretty to look at, but he keeps the mice down in the warehouse. Don't try to pat him, though. He'll scratch you. Oh, you're not allergic are you?" I shake my head.

So many things to worry about, Aunt Gayle.

I reach out for the chunky mug of thick hot chocolate on the solid wooden table in front of me. A marshmallow floats at the top, peeking over the mug. I take a sip.

Marshmallows. Hot chocolate.

I totally forgot about hot chocolate. And let's not

even start on the impossibility of marshmallows.

"All done!" Aunt Gayle flops into the chair across the table, takes a drag of her cigarette, squints at me.

"You look really good, Firefly." Then she reaches across the table and almost places her hand on my arm. But I pull back a fraction before she can touch me. She takes her hand away. Then clears her throat.

"So, here we are."

I nod. It's dark outside. Above the stove, a digital clock glows: 7:45 p.m.

"I guess we should talk, at least a bit."

She looks at me, awkward. Poor Aunt Gayle. Where, oh where, do we start? I think she's hoping I'll say something, but I can't. I mean really. What do I say to start this conversation?

Sorry, sorry, sorry? Where have I been for the past six years? Who am I? What am I doing in your kitchen? Do you even remember me?

What would Joanne-the-mother say? A rant about privilege and wealth. Not where I'm going to start.

"I mean, we should probably talk about a few things. But we'll go slow, okay? Just what you're ready to talk about," Aunt Gayle offers.

I look out the window. To the street. What did the therapists at Jennie's always say? Name things you can see. Ground yourself. Breathe.

Take a breath, Firefly.

I see that the streetlights are on.

I see the Shoppers Drug Mart sign on Queen Street, to the south.

A plastic bag swirls past the parking lot in front of the shop.

The trees are almost bare.

A man in a bright red jacket walks past on the sidewalk.

"Firefly? Okay?"

I nod.

"Yeah. Okay."

Aunt Gayle takes a drag of her cigarette, and I reach out for one. I point at her pack. Hey. If we're going to talk, I'm going to smoke. Even if I hate smoking.

"Can I have one?"

Aunt Gayle looks shocked. "No, you cannot." Then she reconsiders. "Well, okay. I mean … does your mother … I mean … do you smoke? Really?" She looks so horrified that I can feel a smile somewhere deep. I let it come. A little grin.

"Naw. Not really. I mean, I do smoke. But I don't *like* it." She looks puzzled, but she pushes the package across the table toward me. I light one, draw a light drag, put it in the ashtray beside hers. Try not to cough. Two twin smoke trails entwine to the ceiling.

She takes a deep breath.

"Don't tell the social worker. So, Firefly. I've been trying to think of what to say. And I think the only thing

I want to say right now is you're welcome here, I want you to know that. I said yes right away when the social worker called last night and asked if you could stay with me." I look up at the ceiling. I reach out and pick up my cigarette, puff, put it back down.

I really hate smoking.

Aunt Gayle soldiers on. She has deep brown eyes, expressive.

"I'm sorry about everything, Firefly. I mean it. I'm sorry I didn't know what was going on with your mother. With you. I tried to keep in touch with her, but Joanne changed her number all the time. I sent a birthday card for you last year; it came back undeliverable." She glances at me. Awkward shifting of her butt in the chair. Another drag.

"She went through a lot of burner phones," I say. "And we moved a lot."

Aunt Gayle nods.

"Well, yes. No doubt." She hesitates, then takes a breath.

"I care about your mother and you, even if we've been out of touch. She's my little sister. You're my niece. I should have helped somehow, checked in with you, but whenever she did call, she told me everything was okay." Aunt Gayle pauses, her voice trailing off.

This is harder than she was expecting, I think. My eyes slide over to Juggers, who's crouched at his bowl, dozing. Don't eat everything at once, save some for later. His wrecked face is actually quite beautiful. Orange and tousled.

But I've seen plenty of ruined beauty; best not to get too close until you know each other better.

Aunt Gayle heads bravely on. "What I'm trying to say is, I failed you." She looks away fast, blinks hard. "And I'm sorry. I'm glad you're here with me now, though. We'll fit. Okay?"

I nod. Aunt Gayle moves a stray piece of hair out of her eyes. For a second, I see Joanne-the-mother. They really do look alike; they really are sisters. How weird.

"You can stay with me, for as long as it takes."

Yes. That's the thing. How long is it going to take? How long *does* it take, Aunt Gayle? I sip some hot chocolate, nibble marshmallow.

Juggers shoots me a look, then his green eyes close and he goes back to eating. He looks like he hasn't eaten in a while, either. Or no, that isn't quite it. He looks like he knows what it's like not to eat. The possibility of not eating.

Stray cat, stray cat, where your kitty-katty home be at?

Moss Cart sings this (there's more but I can't remember it) every time a misguided cat tries to convince him to let it live with him in the park. But he always takes them in until they get tired of living in a shopping cart, and take off. He's like St. Francis with animals. They can't leave him alone.

I drain my mug of hot chocolate.

"You look like Joanne, Aunt Gayle," I say finally. "Really, quite a bit." My aunt smiles, relieved that I've said something. It gives her strength.

"School starts on Monday, Firefly. You're not going to lose any more time at school. Unless you really don't want to go? I know Joanne was intending to home school you through high school, but I won't be able ..."

"No, school is fine," I blurt out. Wow. Grade nine, after all. Aunt Gayle looks relieved.

"The social worker is organizing everything. She'll get your school files sent over from last year. I've told her about the school around the corner. So, you'll be going to Leslie Street Central starting Monday. Amanda went there, it's a nice school. Not too big. Not too insufferably small, either."

I blink. Good word. Insufferably.

Not too *insufferably small*.

"Anyway, tomorrow we can go shopping for whatever you need. And you can just take your time, okay?" Aunt Gayle smiles. "All the time you need, Firefly."

And that's pretty much how I spend the first night of my new life with Aunt Gayle.

Clean. Fed. Braided. Smoking. Reminded of marshmallows. Sitting in her kitchen. Surrounded by seven million film and television costumes, in an enormous warehouse.

And not at all living with her sister, Joanne-the-mother. My mother.

Or as I call her, Joanne-the-mother-in-the-house-across-the-park.

THREE

Sharlene Baker

I can't fall asleep.

I lie on the bed, stare at the ceiling, listen to the sounds of east-end Toronto outside the window. Across the parking lot, the Queen streetcars rattle and rumble by all night. Which is comforting. There's a clock on the desk, which says it's 1:15 a.m.

1:16 a.m.

1:23 a.m.

1:57 a.m.

Car headlights shoot across the ceiling as people drive through the back alley and into their garages.

I hear sirens. Police. Ambulance. Fire.

People are out there in cars, streetcars, ambulances, and cop cars.

Living, walking, talking to each other, being peaceful or getting into trouble. Living, or dying. Getting high or drunk.

I don't want to complain, but it's surprisingly hard to sleep on a bed again. It's too soft.

And it's too quiet. I'm used to listening carefully for Joanne-the-mother muttering in her sleep or thrashing around in her room.

Or snoring. I miss the snoring. That meant she was sleeping, so I could sleep too. I can't hear Aunt Gayle, which is making me a little uneasy. What's she doing? Where is she? In the apartment? Downstairs? It's 2:13 a.m., so she must be asleep in the room next to me, but I can't hear her.

I consider creeping out of my room and peeking into her bedroom to make sure she's in there …

I drag the big wardrobe in front of the door just in time, before Joanne-the-mother slams it open, swearing. GET ME SOME WATER FIFI! PRIVACY IS A PRIVILEGE! OPEN THE DOOR! SLAMSLAMSLAM! OPEN IT!

I could block the door with the desk. I get out of the bed and start dragging the heavy desk over the carpet, then stop.

I stare at the door, at the desk, at the bed.

What am I doing? I'm not in Joanne-the-mother's house. Aunt Gayle probably doesn't want me to drag the furniture around this room. Even I can see that's probably a little questionable. It's going to take me some time to get used to this.

I hear one of the therapists at Jennie's: *Breathe, Firefly.*

I take a deep breath.

I drag the desk back to its spot beneath the window.

Then I give up on the bed and crawl onto the carpeted floor. I've slept on the floor plenty in my life; no one looks for you on the floor. You can get out the door faster, too, if you have to. I pull the blue comforter over me … and wake up to Aunt Gayle gently knocking on the door. Sunlight streams in the window. The little clock on the desk says it's 10:45 a.m.

This shocks me. I did sleep!

"Firefly? Are you …?"

The door opens a crack, and I wave at my aunt from my nest on the floor. She does a good job not reacting. She doesn't, for instance, ask, "Why are you lying on the floor?" which would be reasonable enough. I'm suddenly thankful I didn't drag the desk over to block the door last night. That would have been difficult to explain.

But she doesn't do anything except look at me.

Then she says, "Breakfast? Scrambled eggs and bacon? Toast? Do you drink coffee? Or tea?"

I blink. Sit up. Rub my eyes.

"Yes. Please. Coffee. That all sounds good."

Aunt Gayle closes the door, and as soon as she's gone,

I rustle down the hall to the bathroom.

Running water, first thing in the morning.

No more sneaking into the house to use the bathroom, or holding it until I can make it to Tim Hortons. Or school.

I can definitely get used to this.

Aunt Gayle has also left a new toothbrush and toothpaste for me on a clean towel on the table outside the bathroom. There's a hairbrush, too.

Not bad, Aunt Gayle.

I revel in pump hand soap, the miracle of toothpaste. I undo my braids and brush my hair out. Then I throw the fluffy gray bathrobe from yesterday over the blue Queen's track pants and *My Little Pony* T-shirt and wander downstairs.

There are two people in the kitchen.

Aunt Gayle is standing at the stove, but turns to look at me. She looks like she needs a cigarette.

And the social worker from yesterday, the one who brought me here, is sitting at the table.

I blink at them. I cannot for the life of me remember the social worker's name.

Sharon? Carina? Kathleen? It was kind of hard to pay attention yesterday, I guess.

"Hello, Fifi. It's Sharlene Baker. Good to see you this morning."

Sharlene Baker is dressed in a big-shouldered suit.

Clearly no one in her life has the guts to tell her it's from the eighties. She's got a clipboard on her knee. I shoot a look at Aunt Gayle, who gives me a quick, raised-eyebrow smile. *Is this really what social workers wear these days?* we're both thinking. Juggers slips past her foot. Gone like smoke, into the costume shop. Coward.

"It's Firefly."

Fifi. The sound of my real name in Sharlene Baker's mouth makes me want to hurl. I've always hated my name: Fee-Fee. It's a poodle name, plenty of kids were happy to tell me that. The singsong of it makes me wants to start yapping like a poodle. I've done it.

I sit down, and Aunt Gayle drops a plate of scrambled eggs, bacon, and toast in front of me. I pour myself a full glass of orange juice. Try not to shake. This is the social worker who *would not shut up* yesterday in the car.

She was the one who was there when everything happened.

The one who nabbed me.

"Sleep okay, Firefly?" Aunt Gayle asks me. She comes over to my side of the table, takes the chair next to me. The two of us look across at Sharlene Baker.

My aunt has her arms crossed.

"Yeah. The bed was really comfortable," I say, and my aunt smiles. I tuck into the bacon and eggs. For the next five minutes, I don't say a word. I eat. I drink orange juice. I drain two cups of coffee. But it's horrifying.

Sharlene Baker talks and talks, asking question after question from the clipboard on her lap.

How old am I?

Thirteen.

When's my birthday?

December 6th.

When's the last time I went to school?

Last June.

Do I have any siblings that I know of?

Geez, lady.

Do I have any contact with my father?

Who?

When was the last time I saw a doctor?

Uh …

A dentist?

Wow.

A school counselor?

A what?

Are my immunizations up to date?

Isn't that something the school should know?

Can I read?

Okay, just stop.

Can I write?

Really, stop.

Do I have a police record or have I ever been arrested?

Stop, now.

Have I ever been in foster care before?

What?

Do I have any STDs that I'm aware of?

STOP!

The dizzying list goes on and on, and Aunt Gayle takes bullet after bullet for me.

She says things like, "Now's not the time to ask Firefly that," about five times in a row. She says, "No, we won't be doing that," a few times too. She answers or she doesn't. She shrugs, waves questions away.

Once she even gets out of her chair a little, places one hand on the table, and stabs a pointer finger at Sharlene Baker with the other. She says, "There is NO WAY she is giving you blood, or having a physical right now. That's not even happening, so don't ask again."

The only thing we say yes to, in unison, is if I know where the local school is. I don't know, but I feel like I have to join in. Show a little solidarity.

"Okay, we can do a more thorough intake in a few days when you're more settled." Then Sharlene Baker snaps her briefcase closed, or tries to and fails because it's so stuffed. So she clamps it under her arm, gets up, and stomps off. She'll be back, clearly, but at least she gets my name right when she leaves.

"Bye, Firefly," she says. "I'll call next week, but you can both call me if you need anything right away. If you can't reach me, leave a message or call the number on the message. It's a real line, a real person will answer and get your message to me." She drops her business card on the table, picks up her briefcase, and spins toward the door.

Then Aunt Gayle sees her out, and I watch as Sharlene Baker's sensible, blue, four-door sedan zips past the kitchen window and careens right on Carlaw Avenue.

That was the car that drove me here. That was the car.

Aunt Gayle comes and pulls her cigarettes out of a drawer, lights up, and offers me one. I shrug and shake my head.

I don't really smoke, Aunt Gayle.

But thanks for asking.

FOUR

Sunday

The first full day with Aunt Gayle is calm.

So calm.

After Sharlene Baker drives away, we drink more coffee, and we don't talk about the fact that Aunt Gayle was like an invisible shield between me and the social worker.

My Warrior Aunt.

That was a lot of questions and I couldn't. I just can't. Not right now. Not yet.

After we have coffee, Aunt Gayle says, "I have a little paperwork to do in the office, then we can go shop for clothes and whatever you need. Okay?" I nod, and she drifts off to the office beside the front door. She shuts the glass door and goes on her computer.

I can see her in there, typing away, cigarette after cigarette burning to nothing.

I wander around. Time for a little investigation.

The shop has a wide countertop beside the front door. Above the door, there's a sign in beautiful hand-written script: *The Costumer is Always Right.*

Cute.

There's an old-fashioned cash register on the counter. I touch a few buttons, but nothing happens. Behind the counter there's a long, low table with a measuring tape glued to it, and four different kinds of scissors on it. Long, thin scissors. Short, curved scissors. Fat-bladed scissors.

Lots of scissors. Beneath the table, there are dozens of boxes on low shelves. Boxes of thread. All kinds of thread, different colors and thicknesses. Boxes of buttons — big, little, cloth, leather, bright rainbows, puffy, white, black, pearly, rosettes, glass, plastic, gold, fabric … buttons, buttons, buttons.

There are needles everywhere, too. Not syringes, which is a nice change from the park, but needle-and-thread needles in every possible size and thickness. There's one needle that looks like a kid's toy. It's about as long as my forearm and has a huge eye in it.

There's tape with handwriting on the underside that says, "Horse Hair/Weaving Needle."

Weird. Horse hair?

A box of measuring tapes, all carefully rolled. Scraps of material in cloth bags, stored under the table. Balls of wool in a bin, a long, thin box of knitting needles beside it. Dozens of knitting needles in the box. Dozens.

Glue sticks. A hot glue gun. A box of rhinestones that I shake gently, then open and my magpie heart thrills a little. There's another box marked "Fake gemstones." A box of "feathers, real and fake." A shelf of weird stuffed birds, lace, hat pins, and ornate gems that says "Fascinators."

I take a look at the far wall of the workshop, and there are more shelves, with more boxes. Boxes that run around the outside of the shop floor, right up to the ceiling.

There's too much to look at. Just hundreds and hundreds and hundreds of boxes filled with costume supplies to create any kind of costume you could ever, ever want. There's lace. More buttons. Hemming material. Patches. Necklaces. Costume jewelry. Rings. Belts. Rubber molds for masks, or hands or feet.

Then there are the rows upon rows upon rows of costumes hanging on the racks, floor to ceiling, two stories high.

I have to look away and calm down. There's just *so much* in here. You could be anything, anybody, from your wildest dreams.

I open the double doors of an enormous closet.

It has hundreds of hanging pocket racks, all the pockets labeled. Pockets marked sunglasses. Reading glasses. Lorgnettes (which is two tiny lenses). Monocles (which is one lens). Then sub-sections. Aviator sunglasses. 1950s sunglasses. Ladies' reading glasses. Men's. Kids'. Colorful. Wire. Plastic. Antique.

On and on and on. It's mesmerizing. Obsessive. You could sort forever in here. I haven't even started looking at the thousands of racks of costumes.

Seven million pieces.

Part of me starts to feel a little panicky. I know hoarders. Lots of the ladies at Jennie's hoard, or did when they still had homes. Now they hoard whatever is left to them in their cart or sometimes in a chain of them.

Moss Cart hoards what he can in his shopping cart. It's his only control over the world.

Stuff. But in particular, *his* stuff, carefully selected and placed in a very particular way that nobody should mess with. I never do. If he ever asks me to get something for him from his cart (a clean pair of socks, for instance), I just smile and politely say no. Unless he really needs me to, anyway.

I learned that lesson early. I accidentally moved a soccer ball of his once without asking. Just picked it up because ... well because I wasn't thinking and I didn't know him very well yet and it was clean, and right there on the top of the cart.

He started crying.

I wonder, just for a second, what Moss Cart would think of The Corseted Lady? He who spends hours organizing and re-organizing the clothes, books, cosmetics, boxed granola bars, juice boxes, and other essentials in his *My-Little-Pony*-covered shopping cart. I get a sudden pain behind my eyes.

He'd never get out of here alive.

Hoarding wasn't one of Joanne-the-mother's problems, though. She sold everything. By the end of the summer, her house was almost empty.

I wander through the shop a little more. There are three antique, over-stuffed couches beside an ancient piano near the front door of the shop. A suit of armor — it's not real armor, I discover with a little plunge of disappointment — guards the front door beside the piano. There's an umbrella stand stuffed with Mary Poppins-looking umbrellas. Beside that is a tall, beautiful statue of a rooster, for some reason.

I must have seen all of this last night when I followed Aunt Gayle upstairs. But I didn't take any of it in. It's like I'm seeing all of it for the first time.

I bounce up and down in one of the couches, and it's comfy. The whole place is kind of well-used, but classy. Built for comfort. And sorting clothes into obsessively labeled groups.

Seven million pieces make me uneasy, though I'm not sure why.

Juggers slinks out of the darkness of the costume racks and crouches, eyeing me.

"If you catch any mice, cat, don't bring them to me."

Stray cat, stray cat, where your kitty-katty home be at?

I get up and walk past a whole rack of clown costumes, which make me shudder. There's a rack marked "Halloween" with a lot of weird, colorful, lumpy costumes in bags. Behind them is a rack of Santa suits and elf costumes. Beside that is a rack of monk cloaks and nun's habits. Then a rack of broken-down clothes with a label that says, "Hoboes, Urchins, Street People."

I rush past, then go and have the second bath of my new life.

Which is twice as many baths as I've had in months.

FIVE

Beloved Baby Soccer Balls

We don't go shopping.

I just couldn't do it. Aunt Gayle stopped working a few hours later, and she came and asked me what I wanted to do, what I needed, and honestly I just couldn't tell her that I needed anything.

What do I need? What do I want? I have no idea.

But one thing's for sure, I've never, ever wanted to go shopping. I've been finding second-hand clothes for myself from Jennie's for almost a year now, I just can't imagine pulling new clothes off racks in an overly bright store, then submitting to the horrors of a change room and a perky salesperson.

Instead, I find a good, artfully ripped (*expensive*) pair of jeans in the pile of Amanda's clothes that Aunt Gayle left on the bed. She folded all my clean stuff from

Jennie's on the chair in the bedroom, so I grab a gray T-shirt (probably once white, but nothing to do with Aunt Gayle's laundry skills), and my black, zippered AC/DC hoodie.

I found this hoodie at Jennie's at the beginning of the summer, and I haven't gone a day without it. Although, what's AC/DC exactly? A band, I think? Or something to do with electricity? Not sure.

I tell her, "I'm sorry, Aunt Gayle. I'm not really up for shopping today."

And she says okay. And she doesn't make a big deal about it, and instead we walk through the neighborhood so I can find my way around.

It's the third week of October, so it's not too cold. Not too hot. Hoodie weather.

This part of Queen Street East is trendy. There are so many stores, I can't keep track. There are food stores and specialty food stores, bars, then specialty bars that serve liquor like just wine or just scotch, which I tried once because Moss Cart had a bottle, and it is truly disgusting. Lots of Starbucks coffee places (I count four in as many blocks), but some nice little family-run coffee places, too. There's a library with an ornate front door and I peek inside. I'll be back.

Librarians don't mind if you use the bathroom or take a nap for a while in an overstuffed chair. Just make sure you're holding a book.

We walk along, mostly quietly, as I take in the neighborhood in my carefully ripped, second-hand jeans and AC/DC hoodie. My hands are stuffed in the pouch, right where I can keep them safest. There's a lot to see. I'm quiet but watching.

At lunch time, we have burgers at Aunt Gayle's favorite local pub, where everyone seems to know her.

It's called The Royal Fox. She introduces me as her niece, Firefly, and everyone says "Hey, Firefly" and no one asks any questions. I get the feeling that Aunt Gayle is their favorite customer, since they are quick to bring our lunch, and as people leave or come, they almost all stop to say hello to her and get introduced to me.

Everyone is really pretty nice. No one asks any embarrassing questions, like "Why are you staying with your aunt?" or "Where are you from?"

Which is good, because I'm really not sure what I would say if they did.

I'm staying with Aunt Gayle because I have to.

I'm from the park across from my mother's house.

After lunch, we walk around the neighborhood some more. We walk east on Queen, then cross Leslie Street and head north two blocks. Aunt Gayle is good company. She's been quietly telling me a little about the business — the kind of film and television customers she gets, the latest movies she's been working on — and I listen, impressed. But honestly, it's been so long since

I've seen a movie or television that I can't tell her I know what she's talking about.

I don't. I don't know any of the actors or shows. We haven't had a working television or a computer for a long time at Joanne-the-mother's house. For the last little while, at the end of the summer anyway, we didn't have electricity either because she stopped paying the bills, so it wouldn't have mattered if the television worked.

I have some serious catching up to do here.

We stop in front of Leslie Street Central High School.

It's a big, red brick building with white trim around the windows and doors. A Canadian flag blows on the flagpole in the October sunshine. A bunch of high school boys are playing soccer, or maybe it's soccer practice. I'd guess it's a school team thing, judging by the identical purple shirts and the coach with a whistle yelling at them.

A boy winds up and boots the ball. It sails straight at me.

I duck.

It flies over where my head just was and rolls out into the street. The annoyed-looking boy trots past us to get it.

His knees, his broad shoulders, his clean, carefully trimmed hair. Everything about him screams *normal*. I can barely look at him as he trots back to the pack of boys in identical shirts and shorts.

I feel edgy and dirty. I pull my hood up, tie it tight.

Then we walk around the outside of the school. I see the front door, the gym through the window, the sturdy, 1910 engineering of the place. We walk through the large side field ringed by huge trees, through the parking lot, then we wander into the quiet, urban neighborhood. People pull cars into driveways. They unpack groceries. They set up hockey nets in the leafy street, or kids take slap shots at garage doors.

This is almost *too* normal. And none of it is normal for me.

I understand that tomorrow I am to start school for the first time since June, weeks after everyone else. And it's high school.

Moss Cart has his soccer ball in his shopping cart, wrapped in a pink blanket. He calls it Baby. Talk to Baby, Firefly. I hold Baby, talk to Baby. Hello, sweet Baby. How are you today, sweet Baby? Is Daddy taking good care of you, Baby? Moss Cart takes her back from me, cuddles her … she's a girl, I think … places her lovingly back into his shopping cart.

I have come to a stop. I'm standing perfectly still in the middle of a small park. Kids swing nearby. I hear them shriek. Aunt Gayle is right beside me, staring into my face.

"Firefly? Did you hear me?" She looks a little worried, and I come back. I shake my head.

"Sorry. It's been, you know, a while. School, I mean. I'm a little nervous, I think." Aunt Gayle nods.

"Of course you're nervous. New school, grade nine. I can't say it'll be a breeze, but the kids at that school are okay. It's downtown Toronto. Anything goes."

"Aunt Gayle?"

She stops. I can hear the kids behind me shrieking, swinging. Carefree. They have never held beloved Baby soccer balls, I'm betting. She raises her eyebrows. "What, Firefly?"

"What exactly are we going to tell the principal tomorrow? About why I'm starting school late? Like, what do we say?"

Aunt Gayle considers me. She takes a drag of her cigarette, then drops it and grinds it under her heel. The sky gets darker, splatters of rain gust across the park. A few leaves blow by. It's suddenly colder. She pulls her coat around her. She told me it's a red barn coat — super urban looking.

She looks at me with the most interesting look. Caring. Considering. Aunt Gayle is figuring it out.

"We tell the principal whatever you want, Firefly," is what she says.

I nod. "Okay. The truth would sound stupid."

Aunt Gayle looks at me, then looks down at her feet. "Well, it wouldn't be stupid, whatever the truth is. I imagine the principal at this school has heard a lot of different things from kids. It's a very diverse neighborhood, kids from all over the world and lots of different cultures, and probably lots of kids get home-schooled for a while ..."

Watching the high school kids crossing the park. New backpacks, new school clothes ... I hide behind the bushes, so no one will ask. No one will see me with Moss Cart, because no one looks at him, although I'm barely recognizable these days anyway, even if they did look at me.

I shake my head and a bunch of stuff blurts out of me, fast.

"I wasn't going to be home-schooled. I made that up. There wasn't money for school supplies or clothes, or anything. High school makes you pay for a locker, a gym outfit, hot lunches, all kinds of stuff. I got a letter at the house in August, with all the fees laid out."

I stand perfectly still, surrounded by my hoodie. The truth just hangs there.

Please don't hug me Aunt Gayle.

But she doesn't. Instead, she bites her bottom lip. Then she sighs.

"That doesn't sound stupid. We'll come up with something for the principal tomorrow. You were overseas working with orphans. You were up north planting trees with a youth group. You were ..."

"Stop!" I say, raising my hand. But I do smile, just a little. Aunt Gayle is keeping it light. I like that.

Then we head back to The Corseted Lady, place of seven million costumes, for grilled cheese sandwiches and a night of television.

Another bath. More braids, hot chocolate, and marshmallows.

So many ordinary things to get used to.

SIX

School, Day One

*D*on't say another word, or you get this. *Joanne makes a face, grabs my thigh under the table at the yard sale, squeezes hard. My pudgy little girl leg throbs and there's a red hand mark on it … I was just saying to the lady that she was buying my old tricycle … I'm six, I think.*

Joanne-the-mother always had a thing about my bikes, though. On the last day of grade eight, I walked home and my bike was sitting beside the sidewalk, with a sign on it: $30. One more thing of mine Joanne decided to sell off. I wonder what for that time? Rent? Drugs? Some tallboys from the beer store?

I removed the sign. Joanne-the-mother neglected to lock the bike. Maybe she sold the lock first? I wheel the bike to the park and dump it in the bushes behind the bench.

Here's a bike for you, Moss Cart …

The principal, Mrs. Hazelle, has just asked me a question. She's looking at me, waiting for an answer. Aunt Gayle is sitting beside me, also looking at me. Light streams in the high windows behind the principal.

"Um, sorry. I'm not sure what you asked me?"

Mrs. Hazelle and Aunt Gayle exchange a look. How long did I just vanish? Why was I thinking about stupid bicycles and Joanne-the-mother?

"Mrs. Hazelle was asking if you want to take art or music as your art credit?"

I blink. I'm wearing the expensively ripped jeans from yesterday and my AC/DC hoodie, with a faded green neon shirt underneath. The shirt has a picture of a baby in a diaper dancing, with the words "Stewie Griffin" on it. A television character, Aunt Gayle told me. I pick at the careful rip in the jeans. This rip could be a *lot* more realistic.

"Art? Or music?" I hear myself saying. The truth is, I'm stalling. I have no idea what I'd prefer. How am I supposed to know? Beyond finger-painting and recorder in public school, I have no experience with either.

But the bigger truth is, I keep fading out.

I just can't keep my head here, in this sunshiny office. It's warm, and I'm sleepy. I keep drifting off. It's about time for a Tim Hortons coffee run. The principal doesn't have any awkward questions for us, at least the ones I've been present for, since Sharlene Baker has already talked to her. There's a file on the desk with my name on it.

Warren, Fifi.

Mrs. Hazelle tells us this as soon as we sit down.

But really, all these questions are awkward. Art? Music? English? History? Library group?

I must look lost because Aunt Gayle says, "Does she have to decide right now?"

The principal shakes her head and says, "You can let me know tomorrow, if you prefer, Fifi."

I'm about to say *it's Firefly* for the third time when my aunt does it for me.

"You know, she really prefers Firefly. If you wouldn't mind, please put that on the documents, at least the class lists, so she doesn't have to explain her name and correct her teachers all week …"

Mrs. Hazelle nods, turns to her computer and types something quickly. A few moments later the nice lady from the office outside knocks, and comes in with a folder. Mrs. Hazelle hands it to me.

"Okay, Firefly. Here's your schedule, and your classroom numbers. You can come and see me anytime," she says politely. I think she actually means it. The file folder says "Warren, Firefly" on it.

Aunt Gayle writes a check for all the fees: sports, clubs (whether I join them or not), locker fee, hot school lunch on Fridays, and a donation to the Student Council plus a few other things. She hands the check over: $325.

I feel sweaty and guilty making Aunt Gayle pay so much money just for me to go to school.

Then the principal stands up, meeting over. She shakes our hands, and we leave the office. I say goodbye to Aunt Gayle at the front door of the school. There's no one around, since I'm late for first class.

"You going to be okay?" she asks. I'm not sure what I look like, but my aunt looks like she wants to swoop in for a quick hug. I try to stand apart from her and she doesn't do it. She does the hair-braiding at night, she hasn't tried to hug me yet, and I don't really like being touched. She went out and bought me a backpack early this morning, and it's loaded with paper, pens, pencils, erasers, a calculator, a binder. It's heavy and overstuffed, so it would be hard for her to get too close for her hug, anyway.

We stand close, though.

"No one likes high school, Firefly. Anyone who tells you that is lying, or has forgotten what it's really like. I'm two blocks away at the shop. Come home for lunch, we'll deconstruct the morning."

"Okay." Home. *Deconstruct.*

"And if that social worker shows up, Sharlene whatever, just tell her she doesn't have our permission to talk to you without me present. Unless of course you want to talk to her, which is fine, too." She smiles a little (although if she's trying to be reassuring, she's failing because she looks as scared as I probably do), then she races out of the building. She's wearing jeans, chunky heels, and that red barn coat. She looks fantastic, racing down the street toward The Corseted Lady, cigarette smoke trailing behind her.

My aunt is a fire-breathing dragon.

I wander back to the office, get directions to my first class, then take myself there and lurk outside the door. Class has already started. I sweat, try to breathe, knock on the door.

The youngish teacher looks at me through the little window in the door, then opens it.

"Hi. I'm late. Sorry, I'm new." I think I meant to say, hi, I'm new. Sorry I'm late.

I'm pretty rattled here, but the teacher just swings the door wide and says hello.

I walk into the room, and do not look up at everyone. They're all looking at me, but I just hand him my file, which he opens, reads quickly, takes out a sheet and adds it to a pile on his desk.

He hands the folder back to me.

Then I sit at the desk he points out to me. "Over there please, Miss Warren."

It's in the middle of the last row, furthest from the door.

I sit in this desk. Kids sit in the room all around me, working quietly. A few stop, look up at me, then keep working.

And my heart.

What's wrong with my heart?

It's racing. Squeezing. Fluttering. Shooting stars into my head.

I hate being furthest from the door. There's no way to make a speedy exit, if I have to. At least, impossible to make a speedy exit without anyone noticing. I start to feel locked in place. I grip the desk with my hands. I try to take a deep breath. I haven't sat in a classroom in a long time, since the end of grade eight last spring.

I'm not sure I can do this.

Breathe, Firefly. I count slowly to ten, then back down to one, another suggestion from one of the therapists at Jennie's. They were always changing, so I never really learned any of their names. Names aren't my strong suit, anyway, to be honest.

Mr. Somebody is writing on the board.

I see a blackboard at the front of the class.

I see trees outside the window.

The kid in front of me is wearing a red plaid shirt.

His hair is jet black.

Then Mr. Somebody tells everyone to turn their books to page eighty-eight, and there's a general swoosh of turning pages.

Mr. Somebody comes over to me, smiles nicely, and puts a book in my hands. Quietly he says, "Welcome to grade nine math, Miss Warren. Nice to have you here."

Am I, though? Am I here?

And math? I thought I was in English class.

At least somebody knows where we are.

SEVEN

Stewie Griffin

Math goes pretty badly, but honestly, not worse than I was expecting. I keep looking over at the door, at the clock, out the window. I wonder if I can ask to move closer to the door tomorrow, but how would I explain that?

I don't ask, and just sit and sweat.

But Mr. Olmstead (Mr. Somebody has a name) is quite nice in the end and spends a bit of time sitting with me during class.

It's actually not that hard, I realize. I'm not that far behind — they are still reviewing work from last year. And I remember, as I look at the numbers, that math is something I was pretty good at.

But really, math at my senior elementary school last spring seems like a brief moment in someone else's life.

The nice thing? Mr. Olmstead doesn't try to introduce me to anyone. I don't get asked to stand at the front of the class. There's no, "Class, this is Firefly Warren. Please welcome her with a big, Leslie Street Central High School hello."

Or something horrifying.

No. The class got to work doing math, and there weren't even that many glances in my direction. Frankly, pretty much no one cares that there's a new girl sitting in their classroom. Maybe new kids show up at this school all the time?

The other kids are all very hip-looking. There's a cross section of kids from all over the world sitting here; we're from everywhere. There are kids with purple hair and nose rings, kids with hair to their butts, kids with their hair covered, or shaved off. We look pretty urban, busy and engaged. No one really stands out, to be honest.

There's one girl a few desks over who gives me a good stare, but that's about it. Frankly, grade nine kids are the least of my worries.

I do math, although I'm rusty. I don't bother asking Mr. Olmstead to move me, I'll have to deal with sitting so far from the door. As I get busy thinking about fractions, I forget about being panicky. Math will do that to a person.

After class, I get lost and spend half an hour not finding my next class, which is supposed to be Geography. But the truth is, I'm in no hurry. I haven't had to hurry to be anywhere for months, it's hard to get back into the habit. When the geography class must be half over and I'm too late to make an appearance without having to knock on the door and disrupting the class, which I'm not doing again, I realize it's almost lunch time. I have a locker, which I visit, dump my math book and binder.

Then I wander along Queen Street back to The Corseted Lady. It's a blustery day, the leaves are all rattling down the street, across the streetcar tracks, shooting around people's boots.

I cross the little parking lot outside the shop, open the door, the bell tinkles … and the store is full of people.

I freeze in the doorway, my hands deep in my hoodie pockets.

A man in a bright pink silk shirt and black top hat sits at the piano. He's playing something loudly. A young man and woman look over his shoulder at the sheet music on the piano. They seem kind of impressed.

In front of me, a guy walks past the open door holding what can only be … a carrot suit? I mean, it's definitely a large vegetable of some kind. He smiles and says hi, then wanders past with the leafy orange costume.

A woman sits at the long table behind the counter, holding a pair of scissors. There's a long swath of green cloth on the table in front of her. More leafy vegetables?

There's a young guy off to one side, on a ladder. He's

wearing a tool belt and is way up there near the shop ceiling — changing a light, maybe.

And in a little room to my right, a lady sits by herself, sewing madly. I can hear the sewing machine: *brrrr, brrrr, brrrr.*

My mouth is open.

The place is alive with people. It was so quiet all day yesterday and when I left this morning. There was no one here but Aunt Gayle and me since I arrived on Saturday night. And Juggers, who is nowhere in sight at the moment, I notice.

"Hi, Firefly!" Aunt Gayle comes out of her office.

Then, of course, everyone stops and looks at me standing there, with expectant looks.

I raise a hand, feeble. Heart pounds. I hate being singled out. What has she told them about me? Is it okay that I'm here? I want to turn around and leave, but Aunt Gayle bustles over, and this time, unlike math class, I don't escape the introductions. She takes me to say hello to all her employees. She's the boss, I'm family.

I've never been family before. It's agonizing and all I want to do is run. I try really hard to smile, nod, remember names, but I'm bad at it.

First, I meet Sadie.

She's British, I think. She has an accent, anyway. There are beautiful, tiny, yellow flowers painted on her brown cheeks and around her eyes that move a little when she smiles and says hello. I'm blinded for a moment.

I'm also pretty sure she's holding a giant pea pod, but how do you ask that question?

Whatcha got there? Giant pea pod?

But I do somehow get the words out. "Is that … is that a giant pea pod?"

Sadie laughs. "Yeah! We're fixing costumes returned from a kids' show on TVO. They ripped all the vines off, somehow!"

Then I meet Edward. The young man up the ladder. When Aunt Gayle introduces me from the bottom of the ladder he smiles and waves, "Hello, Firefly!" Then continues whatever he's doing with all those tools up there near the lights.

Then Max. The guy carrying the carrot costume. He's Sadie's boyfriend, helping out before he goes to work somewhere else (didn't catch where).

Then I meet Sylvia. The lady sewing in the back room. Her mouth is full of pins when Aunt Gayle introduces us, so she can't really smile or say anything. She nods her head, raises her eyebrows, and then gets back to sewing.

Brrrr, brrrr, brrrr.

Next, I meet the two people by the piano. They are Gillian and possibly Stuart (by this time, I've stopped being able to take anything in). They're costume and production students from the film course at Ryerson

University, who come in on Mondays. They aren't that much older than me.

Last, I meet Ambrose. The piano player himself, who stands up, sweeps off his top hat and bows low before me. He says in this deeply beautiful voice, "At your service, Mademoiselle Firefly."

He's an actor, not an employee, there for a fitting for a Netflix movie, but the Ryerson students are having a hard time corralling him into the change rooms.

Aunt Gayle tells me this as she closes the door to the kitchen and makes me a grilled cheese sandwich for my lunch. Which is accompanied by a glass of milk and a sliced apple.

I look at my lunch plate a long time.

"Everything okay, Firefly?" Aunt Gayle asks. I nod and eat.

No one has ever sliced up an apple for me. Not ever.

I tell her the morning was okay. I tell her the school seems all right, I had math not English like we thought, but I definitely have English this afternoon. And I managed to somehow miss Geography altogether, by getting lost. She seems to be listening, but people keep rapping on the door, then bursting into the kitchen.

Edward knocks to say he's leaving.

Sadie comes to see if there's another bolt of green material, since the pumpkin costume somehow got separated from its fronds at TVO, too. *What were those people doing to our vegetables?* she asks in a laughing way. Stuart (possibly) barges into the kitchen to say that Ambrose doesn't want to stop playing the piano, and can Aunt Gayle please come.

So she sighs, says goodbye, then heads back to run her amazingly busy shop.

And I head back to school.

I'm late by ten minutes. It's been a while since I've had to care about the time.

I like not caring about the time.

I look into the office, and the nice secretary just smiles and says don't worry about it, and tells me how to get to my next class.

Which *is* English. We're reading Shakespeare. *The Tempest.*

Then after that, there's History. We're studying Canada at War, starting with World War One, 1914–1918.

In both classes, the teachers say "sit anywhere" and I score seats close to the door both times. Which makes it slightly easier to breathe and focus.

Then it's final period, which would be my arts class, but I haven't chosen music or art, so I wait in the office until the friendly secretary can help me again. We're becoming pretty chummy.

I have two choices.

Mrs. Uttman for music. Or Mr. Rabinandrath for art.

When I hum and stall, the nice lady says, "Mr. Rabin-andrath really likes the kids to do interpretive work: symbolic work from your day-to-day life. Some of it is really beautiful."

I look at her for a minute, then say, "I think I'll do music, please."

The secretary gives me a note, and I wander slowly to the music class. I look in the little window in the door. Everyone is playing an instrument. They're pretty terrible. I mean, it just sounds terrible from out here in the hall. The teacher keeps tapping her baton on a music stand and saying, "Okay, one, two, three ..." and then this blare of terrible sound hits me.

Does it matter, I wonder, if I don't go in? I can go next week, right?

I keep on walking down the hall, out the back door, past the older kids hanging around by the parking lot. Then I see something, the first thing all day that makes me pause.

A skinny boy is lying on the ground. A not-so-skinny boy is standing over him.

RRRRIIIIIP.

The not-so-skinny kid reaches down and rips off the skinny kid's shirt.

Just rips it right off him. The kid on the ground puts his hands over his head. His chest is skinny, all ribs, no meat on him at all. He's heaving, gasping, drawing fast breaths, hard. Like he's scared? Or crying?

Or asthmatic, maybe?

Moss Cart ... all ribs. Shirtless, pale, wandering around under the pine trees in the park, moaning and shrieking, mud smeared across his face and bare chest until I lead him back to his shopping cart and find him some clothes. I pull out a gray sweatshirt and help him get it on. He's shaking so hard, we can barely manage. When was the last time you ate something? I ask, but he's all eyes — empty, coming-down eyes. I can't risk getting whatever food I might be able to scrounge from Joanne-the-mother's, since the lights in the house are on. She's still awake. I dig around in his cart, in the food boxes at the bottom, and find a granola bar and a juice box. He's too shaky to open either, so I take off the creepy plastic around the little straw, stab it into the box, hand it to him. He squeezes it too hard and juice goes everywhere, so I take it back and hold it for him. He drinks the whole box, his skin pale in the light ...

"Hey, Stewie Griffin. I'm talking to you."

What?

"What the hell are you looking at kid?" Not-So-Skinny Kid says.

I don't answer, I just stand there in my unzipped AC/DC hoodie, with Stewie Griffin on my T-shirt, dancing in his diaper.

"Well I guess I'm looking at you. Ripping off a skinny kid's shirt."

Not-So-Skinny Kid takes this in. I have no fear. Okay, not of him, anyway.

"What the hell is 'AC/DC'?" he demands.

I shrug. "I have no idea. Honestly, if you know, please tell me. I got it from Jennie's. That's a women's shelter. Named after Jennie Smillie Robertson, Canada's first lady surgeon."

Not-So-Skinny Kid moves toward me with a little grunt of disbelief. Skinny Kid sees his chance and gets up and tears out of the parking lot. He just runs away without looking back. Shirtless. Not-So-Skinny Kid doesn't even watch him go. He's too interested in me.

He takes another step toward me. "You should shut up," he says, threatening. At least I think that's what he's going for. He wants me to think he's scary.

I just stand there. Really? What could you possibly do to me that would scare me, kid?

I'd like to know. Tell me.

The bell rings, and Not-So-Skinny Kid looks at the school. A second later, the back door opens and a few kids spill out. Then a flood of kids come out.

"You didn't see anything," he says. He's trying to be scary, but I just look at him.

I think I smile. Or grin. Or look totally unfazed. I know I raise my eyebrows in an *Oh, really?*

I don't know, but he does seem a little surprised at what I say next.

"I did see something. A big jerk kid, that's you, picking on a short, skinny kid who ran off without his shirt because you ripped it." I point at the ruined shirt on the ground.

Not-So-Skinny Kid actually looks shocked. He knits his brows.

Then I give him a rude gesture, one of those you're not supposed to use in polite company, and walk away. It's not something I'd usually do, but hey, it's been a while since I've done this. I haven't been in school since the spring, and I'm basically feral.

I saunter past him, and he snarls, "What's your problem?"

Really, kid? That's the best you can do?

I could share my problems with you if you really want, but where would I start …

EIGHT

Russian Astrakhan Hat

FIFI! FIFI! Joanne-the-mother staggers across the park, falling, stumbling. People playing baseball, walking the dog, everyone pulls away from her. I slip off the bench, hide behind Moss Cart's shopping cart. She's wearing leopard skin print leggings, her hair is up in curlers ... FIFI! FIFI! Drunk or high? Or just mad at me? Hard to tell. I glide behind a tree, then slip behind the kiddie slide, hide behind the fence, crouching. She stumbles but sees me, and I take off at a run ... last thing I see is Moss Cart standing in her way, trying to talk to her, calm her down. Be cool, lady, *he says in that gentle way of his ...*

I wake up in a cold sweat.

Where am I?

Blue-white moonlight shines through the window onto my face, and I see the CN Tower in the near distance.

I sit up.

I'm lying on the floor of the guest bedroom in the apartment. I'm at Aunt Gayle's, at The Corseted Lady, sleeping under a comforter on the floor.

Right. I draw up my knees and rock a little. Someone drives a car past on Queen Street, and the headlight strafes across the ceiling. I take a few breaths, try to calm down.

Tree. Window. Tree. Light. Desk.

I get up after a while and head to the washroom and the miracle of hot water. It really is a problem, going pee at night when you're hiding in a ditch, or sleeping on a park bench.

Juggers is sleeping on one of the overstuffed chairs in the living room, and wakes to watch me.

We eye each other carefully.

"Don't worry, Jugg-or-not, I won't try to pet you." Something about my tone makes him relax, and he stretches out his front paws. Yawns.

"Well, aren't you all at-home and comfy."

I walk back down the hall, past Aunt Gayle's room. (She's gently snoring, which calms me: she's sleeping, all is well.) Then I open the apartment door and head out into the warehouse.

The costumes are creepy enough by day, but at night it's all I can do not to scream. The empty costumes, all disembodied, that's the word, look really odd, floating in the darkness, suspended from the ceiling.

I brush past the Rolling Judy outside the apartment door, the one with the 19th Century Flower Girl hoop skirt on it (Aunt Gayle called it a "Dickensian Flower Girl" costume when I asked), and carefully avoid touching it. I try not to think of the street urchins from the time, all the poor ones not dressed like this.

I walk along the main hall, through the racks, and there are armless sleeves, and legless pants, and headless hats, and footless boots, and on and on and on. There's a whole world here of emptiness.

Then it hits me what it is that I find so creepy about The Corseted Lady, with its seven million pieces: *all the people in these clothes are missing.*

Aunt Gayle told me last night at dinner (which was that teriyaki-chicken salad she promised) how a lot of the costumes are items she bought at auction. Meaning, sales from the estates of dead people, at least some of the time.

The rest of the costumes she and her staff either made, or got someone to make for them. Like most of the fancy hats are made by a local milliner. A few of the specialty boots are made by a cobbler, which is so old-fashioned I almost can't believe it. Cobblers, in Toronto. Do they wear leather aprons, sitting on those shoemaker benches like in fairy tales?

And so on.

The moon shines into the warehouse, there are floor

to ceiling windows on all the far walls, and the light hits the empty clothes …

… and I get a sudden wave of sadness.

These clothes are memories, shadows of all the people who lived in them. They may have loved these clothes. Like I love my AC/DC hoodie. I've spent a lot of time pawing through boxes and boxes of donated clothes at Jennie's. Not just for something clean to wear, but for something of *mine* to wear. Something about all these clothes hanging, empty, makes me feel sad and kind of rattled.

What would happen if Moss Cart got let loose in here? He'd never stop dressing and undressing. For the rest of his life, he'd just move from rack to rack, trying to choose something to wear.

I wander through the nearest rack. It's a wall of fur coats and then heavy woolen coats. I mean, these are serious winter wear. The fur coats range from "Siberia, 1880s" to "1950s Lady's Neck Wrap." The Siberian wool coats, there are four of them, are beautiful and soft, and huge. You'd be covered from your nose to your boot tops in one of them.

The sign at the end of the rack says "Russian Military, Greatcoats."

I slip one off the hanger and put it on.

It's heavy. And warm, super soft, and beautiful. It's got enormous buttons — they look like bone or something.

I do them up.

There's a shelving unit of winter hats beside the fur coats, and one shelf says "Russian Astrakhan Wool Hats." I pick out a hat and stick it on my head.

There's a full-length mirror nearby, and I catch my moonlit reflection in it.

I look … well, I guess I look like a Russian soldier. The coat is way too long for me, drapes along the ground like a cape behind me, but together with the hat, the whole effect is Russian.

Did someone own this coat? Did he love it? Who was he? I pull the coat around me, take a few more steps in front of the mirror.

A shadow slinks out from under the coats.

Juggers walks to a splash of moonlight on the warehouse floor.

He sits down. And observes me.

"What do you think, Juggers? How do I look?" Juggers flicks his tail, watches, remains silent in the way of cats. But his green eyes shine.

"I think you approve."

I walk in the heavy coat over to the window and look down into the street. It's 4 a.m., so no one is on the street out there. Toronto is quiet on this October night. The CN Tower stands sentinel off to the west.

I haven't been thinking about the boy who had his shirt ripped off him at school today, but suddenly his pale, white chest, heaving with sobs or possibly asthma, pops into my head. I've seen enough people rip off their own shirts and wander around, muttering in the darkness. Moss Cart did it all the time until I showed up in the park and started to convince him to keep his clothes on whenever I could. When she was at her worst, drugged-out self, Joanne-the-mother could wander around mostly undressed, too, not caring where she was or who was watching.

Moss Cart would always let me help him. Joanne would not.

But I've never seen anyone get their shirt ripped off them.

Frankly, it's a level of ugliness I've never encountered.

I haven't been thinking about that bully kid. I roll my eyes under the Astrakhan hat. He's going to be a problem, clearly.

Juggers jumps up onto the window ledge beside me. We both look out into the street below. The Queen streetcar tracks run past, and all the stores are locked up. The big Shoppers Drug Mart still has bright lights on, though. And the liquor store further down the street.

No one around.

"Are you purring, cat?" I lean over a little, the Astrakhan hat slips over my eyes. Yep, the ugly orange cat is purring.

Stray cat, stray cat …

"You know what these clothes need? All these clothes need a little love," I say. And I almost pat the cat's head.

My hand moves toward him, absent-minded. But he vanishes, just a wispy idea of a cat, before I do touch him.

What was I thinking?

But his purring and the clothes and the hat give me an idea.

It's a weird idea, and it just pops in there. And honestly, who knows why?

The moonlight, the CN Tower, the warehouse, the stupid purring cat, the skinny boy's heaving ribs as he lay on the school ground without his shirt, Moss Cart sipping on a juice box with gratitude, the fact that I'm supposed to somehow go to high school, the look on Joanne-the-mother's face when they led us into different cars two days ago (she went to a cop car, I got led away to Sharlene Baker's sensible, blue, four-door sedan) …

… any or all of those things.

But it's an interesting idea.

I look over the rows of costumes.

I can love these clothes like I love my AC/DC hoodie. I found it in a huge jumble of clothes, unloved. I can honor the people who wore these clothes once and those who don't have any clothes or rip theirs off in a drug-induced terror.

Or have their shirts ripped off their backs for them.

I can do what Moss Cart never will: sort through the biggest box of second-hand clothes in existence.

And to love them is to wear them.

NINE ✗

Flyboy

O kay, I can't possibly wear all seven million pieces. I realize that, even as I think it. But I can get to know them. Touch them. Walk among them.

See them.

I settle back to sleep, no problem. This morning, I get up from my nest on the floor when Aunt Gayle taps on my door at 7:30 a.m.

"School, Firefly," she says quietly, then I hear her leave the apartment.

I wonder what's for breakfast?

I have a shower. Although I long to take a bath, I don't have time. Then remember, hey, I can have a bath after school if I want. I get dressed in the expensively ripped jeans, a clean white T-shirt, and walk out into the warehouse. I leave my AC/DC hoodie lying on the bed with its arms wide.

I carefully skirt the Dickensian Rolling Judy and stop at the first row of hangers outside the apartment door.

The orange sign at the end of the row says, "World War I Soldiers & Medical."

I walk along the aisle and stop at "Men's, FLYBOY." My hand brushes across the shoulders of a dozen leather World War One flying ace jackets. Large, medium, small.

My hand hovers over a small, dark blue leather jacket with fake fur at the collar and heavy snaps up the front.

I slide it off the hanger, slip it on my shoulders.

Perfect fit. And it's worn to a soft, leathery perfection.

The jacket has a set of gloves and a flying ace hat with goggles to match, attached in a bag.

I slip the leather hat over my head, slide on the leather gloves.

Whoever this flyboy was, he wasn't big. My size. Was he a teenager? I bet he wasn't fully grown. Did he get to be?

I stop in front of the full-length mirror and inspect. Pretty eccentric.

And perfect.

I saunter into the kitchen, and Aunt Gayle looks up from the table. She's sewing a peace sign patch onto flowery jeans. She smiles, hesitant.

"What are those?" I ask, pointing at the jeans. Then I slide into the chair and make my selection from the cereal boxes lined up in front of my bowl.

Cheerios.

"Um … they're a style from the 1960s. Flower-power bell-bottoms. Happy hippie pants. They're for a CBC documentary on the Summer of Love in Yorkville, 1967. They needed a peace sign, according to the costume designer."

I slurp some orange juice. Taste Cheerios for the first time in … I don't even know.

It's not all that easy to see through the flyboy goggles, which are tinted a dark brown. And the jacket is making me sweat. Aunt Gayle puts her sewing into her lap, takes a drag of her cigarette, looks at me.

"You're in costume today?" she asks, finally.

I nod. "If it's okay with you." This is the only problem with my plan, as I see it. Getting permission. "We're studying Canada at war, World War One at the moment. In History."

My aunt considers. "Okay, Firefly, but that jacket is worth a lot of money. I mean, it's a valuable piece." I stand up and pour myself a coffee. I'm stalling, I really didn't put much value on the jacket, but I guess that makes sense. It's expensive. Especially if it's real.

And I guess it is.

"Uh, you know, it's okay. I should have asked …" I'm about to take off the jacket, but my aunt shakes her head.

"No, wear it if you want to. It looks great on you, actually. Amanda sometimes wore pieces to school, especially around Halloween. How about this: wear whatever you want from the warehouse, but check with me first, okay? Before you go to school, anyway. There are pieces in here that are irreplaceable. I mean, some things I should donate to a museum one day, if I ever get around to it."

I smile, sip coffee, say thank you.

Aunt Gayle, you are awesome.

And that's how I spend my second day at Leslie Street Central: dressed as a World War One flying ace. And I really couldn't give two craps about people looking at me, or smirking, or giggling. Some do, but most don't. And none of the teachers even seem to notice, they just take attendance and start class.

My morning classes begin with Math again. I guess that's my home room, so I have Math every morning, and French. Both classes are okay, although I have to sit far from the door in French class, too, which makes my heart race a little. And because the teacher, Madame Frances, wants us to "live in French," we sit in groups of four. I'm sitting at a desk, with a boy beside me and two girls in desks facing me.

None of us is terribly good at French.

The boy actually makes me grin, though. He says, "Quel joli chapeau," when I sit down.

What a lovely hat. I think so, anyway. I'll have to try to remember his name. Charlie, maybe? The girls just stare at me, and one seems a little worried, but no one is mean. At least not to my face.

Honestly, it's actually fine. Not terrible, anyway.

After Math and French, I slide along Queen Street back to The Corseted Lady for lunch and sit in the kitchen with Sadie eating a tuna sandwich on white bread, which Aunt Gayle left for me. She had to go to a last-minute meeting with a director in Barrie, so she's gone all day.

It's been a long time since I've tasted tuna.

Sadie has brilliant white flowers painted on her cheeks today, and rainbow eye makeup. She tells me that she and Max are slowly traveling around the world. Right now, they live in a Volkswagen Microbus, always on the road.

"What are you doing here, then?" I ask between bites of tuna sandwich. "I mean, you're not on the road right now, are you?"

Sadie laughs. I like her, partly because of the awesome flowers on her cheeks, but also because she doesn't mention the flyboy costume, like it's totally normal to go to school dressed in one-hundred-year-old leathers.

"We stop and work in the big cities and make enough money to keep going on to the next place. We worked in New York City all last spring. Your aunt knows we're only here until spring, then we'll head west and north. I want to see Alaska."

"Uh, you know Alaska is a long way away, right?"

Who am I to burst her bubble? But I also don't want her to fail. Sadie laughs again.

"Oh, I know. It's a month or two driving slowly in the Microbus."

"That's your bus, parked in The Corseted Lady lot?" I've walked past it a few times. It's got flowers painted on it, like the white flowers on Sadie's cheeks. It's beautiful.

She nods. "Your auntie lets us park it there for free. We've lived in the bus for two years now. We crossed most of the U.S. in it."

I frown. "Does it have a bathroom?"

"Yep, although we try not to use it except for emergencies."

"At night," I add, and Sadie nods.

"It's comfortable, Firefly. Come and see it. Knock on the bus door anytime."

I say okay, then head back to school.

Afternoon is: Geography, Science, then Library, which appears to be sitting in a big, comfy chair in the sunshine and reading whatever I want. The other kids with me seem to be doing the same thing, although a few of them are doing homework too. I really don't have any homework yet, so I read. That kid from French this morning — Charlie I think? — is sitting nearby, reading. It might be him, anyway. One girl sits with a teacher at a desk, learning to read.

Or maybe she's learning to read *English*. Yeah, that's it. She's a new Canadian, I guess? She's doing pretty well. They're reading the *Toronto Star* newspaper. The teacher sees me watching, and smiles, then gets back to her student.

I pull a magazine off the wall, *Maclean's*, plop into a comfy chair, and read through it. I can't remember the last time I read a magazine.

No, that's not true. Joanne-the-mother bought you a subscription to OWL *magazine once, when you first moved into the house across from the park. You read it all the time when you were younger, cover to cover, as soon as it came in the mail.*

I frown. Oh *yeah*. I did read *OWL* magazine. How did I forget that?

I get a headache, and suddenly I feel really strange. I'm too hot. I swipe the leather flyboy hat off my head. My heart races.

You sat in the window and read it with Mom, at home, looking down into the park when the leaves were turning color …

I stand straight up, the magazine falls to my feet. I bend, pick it up, put it on the wall rack. I grab the flying ace hat and walk out of the library.

"Wait! Hold up!"

I stop in the hallway. I turn. The teacher stands in the library door.

She walks toward me.

"You okay?" she asks. "You seem a little, maybe not so okay."

"I think so," I say. Then I add, "I'm not sure. I think I should go home."

Home.

"Okay, just sign out at the office. It's Firefly, right? I'm Miss Turner, the library support group teacher. I'll mark you gone home for the day." She smiles again, then turns back to the library.

I find the office, nod to the lady behind the desk, and sign out.

What's *home*?

And who is *Mom*?

TEN

Not-So-Skinny Kid

I walk across the school yard, head south along Leslie Street, then swing west onto Queen Street. I pass the Shoppers Drug Mart and The Royal Fox. Both places have their Halloween decorations up. Spooky paper ghosts are in all the windows along the street, cheap rubber costumes for sale at the pharmacy, spiders and fake webs on door-ways, a pumpkin with a candle in the window of the pub.

I realize Halloween is next week. That hasn't occurred to me until right now.

What else have I been missing?

My hands are deep into the flyboy jacket pockets, I have the goggles pulled down, the leather hat over my ears. I walk slowly toward The Corseted Lady, frowning.

A few leaves blow by on the street. It's a sunny day, but cool.

How could I forget about Halloween? Or how much I loved *OWL* magazine?

I'm not sure what to think. It's hard to hold both the reality of Joanne-the-mother and someone named *Mom* in my head.

There *were* times when Joanne-the-mother was actually a real mother. Sometimes the house had heat, electricity, warm water. We had money and food when she had a job. The last one lasted a while, she was a cashier at the grocery store. I went to school. She bought me a magazine subscription.

I called her Mom.

I gulp. *Take a breath, Firefly.*

Ground yourself. Name things. Stay present to keep from flooding, or drowning, in memories.

I take a look along Queen Street.

I see a lady in a blue coat.

I see a man walking a dog.

The dog is spotted, brown and white. Very cute.

I see a street sign for "Easy Street."

There's a man smoking a pipe.

The man has a beard.

The streetcar is coming toward me.

The streetcar has stopped.

People are getting off.

An older man with a cane is stepping off the streetcar.

There's a boy running down the street toward him.

He looks like he's running for his life.

He is shirtless.

He is being chased.

He's Skinny Kid!

Not-So-Skinny Kid is running after him.

Not-So-Skinny Kid reaches out and grabs him.

Skinny Kid pushes him off, and keeps going.

The old man with the cane has stepped between them.

Not-So-Skinny Kid stops and looks annoyed.

He shouts, "Keep running!" at Skinny Kid. Then he swears, loudly. A few people even notice and look at him then look away.

Skinny Kid gets away, runs around a corner, disappears. Shirtless.

The old man says something to Not-So-Skinny Kid, but I can't hear what because they're on the other side of the street. Not-So-Skinny Kid ignores him, scowls, walks away.

That was ugly.

This is the problem with grounding yourself. Once you decide to notice things, you notice *all* of the things.

And as far as I'm concerned, most of the time all of the things rot.

ELEVEN

Lobster Claws

Today is Friday. What happened to the last three days? I really couldn't tell you.

I do know that after seeing Not-So-Skinny Kid running down the sidewalk after Skinny Kid a few days ago, I kind of fade out. I go to the shop and head to the room in the apartment that is supposed to be mine. I sit for a long time in the chair at the desk, and I look out the window.

What do I think about?

Nothing.

Eventually, I go and have a bath. Aunt Gayle knocks on the door at some point and asks me what I want for dinner.

Pizza? she asks.

Yes, I hear myself say.

I get dressed.

I go and have pizza with Aunt Gayle in the kitchen.

We watch television.

But I couldn't tell you what the pizza tasted like. Or what we watched.

I'm barely here. The therapists at Jennie's said there could be times I might fade out. Is this fading out? How do I know? I do know that for the next three days I eat, I walk to and from school. I must pay attention at least a little because I write a test in Math on Friday morning and pass. I talk to Aunt Gayle and Sadie, and I don't accidentally step in front of a bus or anything.

Part of me must be paying attention, in some way. But the rest of the week is a weird blur.

For someone fading out, I must make a decent display of fading in.

The only thing I really pay attention to, and can remember now, is choosing what to wear each morning. Despite what I wear, I can also tell you that no one, or almost no one, pays very much attention to what I wear. At first the kids barely notice, the teachers too.

And considering some of my choices, you'd think they might, but no.

Here's what I wear to school the rest of my first week at Leslie Street Central:

Wednesday, saloon girl, 1800s. It looks real, but it's not actually from the 1800s. Aunt Gayle made the outfit a few years ago. It's a red dress, with a bustier, a shawl, and these leather boots with a dozen tiny eyes to lace up. It would definitely be a disadvantage to be a saloon girl from the 1800s if you had to get into your boots in a hurry.

If you had to get away fast, for instance.

Thursday, monk, early 1500s. Again, looks real, but totally modern materials. The floor-length cloak, the heavy string tie at the waist, the amazing hood that covers most of my face. I love this costume. This, I could live in. It's really just a bigger version of my AC/DC hoodie.

Friday, medieval warrior. Again nothing about this is real except the way it looks. I've got chain mail leggings on. Well, they look exactly like chain mail but they're knitted from metallic wool and spray painted. Aunt Gayle made them. She knits all the time, her hands are never still. She's an award-winning knitter to make something look so exactly real.

Today is Friday. For some reason, I'm a little more present today.

Less dreamy and faded. I always did like Fridays.

It's medieval warrior day. I've got a chain mail hood and cowl on, also knitted and spray painted to look exactly like chain mail. There's a leather, lace-up soldier vest over a long, white tunic, studded leather boots and heavy leather gloves with armor over the fingers. The spray-painted leggings.

And a broadsword and a shield from the prop cupboard.

(They call it a cupboard, but it's a huge walk-in room, not a cupboard.)

Aunt Gayle scans me over breakfast, then silently removes the broadsword from my hands. Okay, no sword. I get it, can't take a broadsword to school even if it is just a stage prop. I suppose that's sensible, considering the state of the world. Which makes the shield redundant, so I leave that too.

But I still look pretty excellent in the chain mail. I get a lot of looks at school today. In fact, a few kids actually approach me in the hall between classes and ask where I got the Halloween costume (ha!), and I tell them.

My aunt's costume shop. The Corseted Lady.

That kind of thing.

As the week goes on, my teachers grow sweetly interested in what I'm wearing, but it's not a big deal. Mr. Olmstead did note the medieval warrior costume, though. I think he wants one.

I wear my costumes and it's fine. But what's not fine?

Every time I step outside after school — every time — I see the battle between Not-So-Skinny Kid and Skinny Kid.

As Skinny Kid runs for his life along Queen Street, sometimes he's got a shirt on, sometimes he doesn't. Sometimes Not-So-Skinny Kid is close behind, sometimes he's not.

Even in my faded-out, not-very-present state of mind,

I see this shirt-ripping every afternoon. I stop and watch as the two boys run down the street past me.

But that is seriously messed up.

What is it about Skinny Kid that has Not-So-Skinny Kid so worked up?

Why does he think it's okay to rip clothes off another kid?

Why haven't any adults noticed? Other than the old guy with the cane (and honestly, doesn't that mean he's blind or sight-impaired somehow), who said something to Not-So-Skinny Kid a few days ago as he got off the streetcar, I haven't seen anyone else but me even notice the daily ritual. And I'm barely even here.

The ripping of the shirt.

I feel a little helpless about this. I think I should help, though.

But how?

I'm wondering about this, what to do about the situation, as I walk home from school on Friday afternoon. I almost want to find Moss Cart and talk to him about it; he'd have some wisdom. How to stop the ritual ripping of the shirt. But to find him, I'd have to go back to the park.

Across from the house.

What does it look like, now Joanne-the-mother isn't in it? I hope someone turned off the lights and locked the front door after she was driven away in the cop car last week. Someone is going to have to deal with the landlord, who frankly will be very happy to see us gone.

But that someone won't be me.

I'm walking toward The Corseted Lady, wearing the medieval warrior costume. I swing past Shoppers Drug Mart at Carlaw, turn north across the parking lot ... and stop.

Aunt Gayle is standing at the door of the shop. There's a sensible, blue, four-door sedan parked on the street in front.

Aunt Gayle is talking to ... NO! It's Sharlene Baker.

I freeze.

I can't talk to her. I just can't face any more intense, rapid-fire personal questions.

Not now. Not here.

Even though I've been pretty brave today in my medieval warrior costume, I'm not nearly brave enough. I'd rather walk fading in and out through the halls of the local high school dressed as a flyboy, a saloon girl, a monk, a medieval warrior, than talk to the social worker again. Or at least not right now.

I duck behind the Volkswagen Microbus painted with white flowers in the little parking lot beside the shop. Sadie and Max's van. I lean against it. My heart pounds.

I don't feel much like a medieval warrior right now. Or maybe this is exactly how they felt, going off to face the enemy.

I peek around the van, and I hear my aunt raise her voice.

"She's not here at the moment, she's at school."

Sharlene Baker says something back that I can't hear. Then Aunt Gayle says loudly again, "I've told you, I run a business here. It's Friday at 3:30, business hours. You are welcome to schedule an appointment with Firefly outside of business hours, but I will be there."

Sharlene Baker looks at her cellphone, says something.

Aunt Gayle flickers a look over at the Microbus. She knows I'm here!

I think I hear Sharlene Baker say something like, "Can I leave a message for ..."

Then the Microbus door opens a crack and a flowered cheek followed by dark eyes peeks out. Sadie whispers at me, "Psst! Firefly!"

I zip up the two metal stairs and enter Sadie and Max's Volkswagen Microbus.

Sadie closes the curtains on the tiny van window facing the shop. She seats me at a little booth made for two and opens a table that pops up from the wall.

She slides into the booth beside me and says quietly, "They've been at it for a while." She nods toward my aunt and the social worker, arguing at the door of the shop. We can still hear them talking.

I take a deep breath.

"Thanks for rescuing me. Where's Max?"

Sadie smiles. "She's intense, that social worker, almost as intense as your aunt. And Max is at work. He works in a bank."

"He's a bank teller?" I ask.

"He's a cleaner in a bank," she says, smiling. She gets up and opens a tiny fridge and takes out a bottle of fizzy lemon water. She pours some into a cup from a tiny cupboard over the dollhouse sink and hands it to me. Then she takes a box of chocolate chip cookies out of a secret, sliding panel and places it open on the table in front of me.

I take a cookie. I sip the lemon water.

Through the curtains (they're yellow, with tiny red roosters on them), I see Aunt Gayle cross her arms. I see Sharlene Baker cross her arms, too. They both speak, then Aunt Gayle lets Sharlene Baker into the store.

They're gone for now.

I nibble my cookie.

Sadie's phone beeps, and she reads a text message.

"Your aunt says to stay in here, if you want to." She looks up at me. "Do you want to?"

I nod.

There's another beep.

"She asks if there is a time next week you want to talk to Miss Sharlene Shoulder-Pads Baker."

I snort. And Sadie shows me her phone. That's what it says. *Miss Sharlene Shoulder-Pads Baker.*

"Um, no. But if I have to, I guess ... any day after school."

Sadie texts back to Aunt Gayle.

The next text reads, "Wednesday, 8:30. Wave goodbye to Sharlene SP Baker!"

Sadie and I watch as the social worker stomps out of The Corseted Lady, jumps into her sensible, blue, four-door sedan, then drives away. Aunt Gayle waves goodbye to her, then waves hello to us, and goes back into the store. She's followed by a customer with an armload of costumes to return.

Sadie and I wave back.

I nibble my cookie. I sip the lemon water.

"Oh! I wonder if your aunt realizes that next Wednesday is Halloween?"

I shrug. "Does it matter?"

Sadie shakes her head, yes, no. "I guess not. Just I imagine Halloween day is pretty busy in a costume shop. I mean, apparently this weekend, tomorrow especially, is going to be super busy. We all have to work."

"Oh." I suddenly wonder if Aunt Gayle is going to ask me to work tomorrow too. Which is fine, I guess. What else would I be doing?

"What are you going to be for Halloween?" Sadie asks. She picks up a bag from the floor and unfolds a large piece of red material. She lays it out on the table. It's cut into the shape of ... a claw? Now I notice that there are what look like bent red sticks lying on the bed across from me. (It has a comfy pillow, and a bright yellow cover with more tiny red roosters on it, it looks so nice I could take a nap right now.)

"I don't know. I haven't been out for Halloween in years. I'm a little old for Halloween." I nibble. Good cookie.

Sadie rolls her eyes. "No one is too old for Halloween, Firefly. And you basically live in a Halloween wonderland."

I nod. She is so right.

"What are you making?" I nod at the red claw-thing on the table, the bent red sticks on the bed. She is making tiny little stitches along the red serrated edge of the material.

"Oh, your aunt wanted to add another lobster costume to the Halloween rack. So technically, I'm hand-stitching lobster claws. 'I should have been a pair of ragged claws' kind of thing."

I stare at her and she laughs. "Poem. T.S. Eliot. 'The Love Song of J. Alfred Prufrock.' You'll probably study it in English one day. And those," she nods at the red sticks on the bed, "those are lobster legs and stalk eyes. I just finished them."

I barely hear her.

Lobster costume. Wait. What? LOBSTER COSTUME?

"I could be a lobster," I say. "For Halloween, I mean."

Sadie laughs again. She's so sweet. What a great laugh.

"Really? You'd wear a lobster costume to school?" I nod and smile.

"I think so." Then I nod harder. "For sure, I could wear a lobster costume to school. I was a flyboy, then a saloon girl, a monk, and a medieval warrior this week. Who knows what I'll be next week? I kind of like those vegetable costumes, that carrot costume for instance that the TVO production used last week. Why not add a crustacean to the mix? No one at that school pays much attention. It's kind of hilarious."

Then Sadie gets a wicked grin and shakes her head. "What?" I ask.

"Nothing, never mind," she says in a sing-song voice.

I shrug. What could be better than a lobster?

After my cookie and lemon water, I get up, say thanks, and leave.

Two things for sure.

One: I want to live in a Volkswagen Microbus one day. As I was leaving, Sadie showed me the toilet (because I asked), hidden discreetly under the bench I was sitting on.

I almost swooned.

And two: Sadie is the coolest person I've ever met.

Who ever hand-stitched *lobster claws*, or made lobster antennae and legs, while talking to a medieval warrior in a flower-painted, Volkswagen Microbus?

I mean, any one of those things would have seemed like an impossibility for me to utter in a sentence, let alone see in real life, even a week ago.

TWELVE

Firefly, WAKE UP!

WAKE UP! FIREFLY! *A hand shakes me awake.*
They're here! They're looking for you, Firefly. GET UP!

It's Moss Cart shaking me. His shopping cart shines nearby in the dark; the My Little Ponies *look like tiny souls glittering in the streetlight. Where's he been all night?*

I scramble awake, grab my backpack. I didn't mean to fall asleep.

Then suddenly … sirens. Cop car at the edge of the park. Another at the house.

I run, try to get to the house first. Too late.

Joanne at the door. Yelling, YOU CAN'T HAVE MY KID! FIFI! FIFI!

Then Joanne swinging a baseball bat. Cops swirling around her.

A flashlight in my eyes. A hand grabs my arm from behind. FIFI WARREN, are you FIFI WARREN?

I wake up with a yell. Covered in sweat.

My heart hammers.

The clock on the desk says 1:45 a.m.

It's okay, I'm here. I'm on the floor in the blue room at The Corseted Lady. Aunt Gayle is just down the hall. I see a blue comforter. I see a window. I see stars outside. Moon shining. Tree. CN Tower. Tree. Star. Moon. Tree.

Name, name, name things.

The door creaks open.

I hear Juggers jump up onto the bed. He pads across it, then his ugly head peeks over the side of the mattress down at me. I swear the cat raises his eyebrow when he sees me lying there on the floor.

Stray cat, stray cat, where your kitty-katty home be at?

There's more to that song, I can hear Moss Cart singing another line, but I still can't remember it. Juggers blinks, blinks again, then stretches out on the bed and falls asleep.

I realize that I should probably be the one in the bed. But I just can't. It's still too soft and springy. The carpeted floor is actually really comfortable.

I lie for a while in my nest. My heart stops pounding. I listen to the soft snorting of the feral cat on the bed. I toss, I turn. Then I get up and go to the bathroom.

Aunt Gayle is sitting in the living room. The gas fireplace

is on beside her. She's stitching something. Does she knit, or stitch, or sew all the time?

She looks pretty cozy, though. She turns and looks at me.

"Can't sleep?"

I nod. *I could ask you the same thing, Aunt Gayle.*

"You were shouting in your sleep. Bad dream?"

I nod, scratch my arm. *Did I wake her up?*

"Sorry," I mumble.

"Will hot chocolate help?"

I nod again, and head into the bathroom. I hear my aunt leave the apartment and walk through the warehouse then down the rickety wooden stairs to the kitchen. After the miracle of running water and plumbing, I wander into the living room and sit on the big armchair next to the gas fireplace. There's an enormous quilt over the arm and I pull it over all of me, draw my feet up.

Place is cozy, all right.

Moss Cart's voice. The flashlight in my face. Joanne-the-mother screaming at the cops that they can't have me, screaming my name, waving the baseball bat …

It's not a dream. It's all true.

Aunt Gayle comes back with two cups of hot chocolate and a plate of blueberry muffins. She puts them on the coffee table between us. My mouth waters.

"Thanks," I say. My aunt settles back into the couch, picks up her stitching.

"What are you working on?" I ask.

"Oh, you know, Halloween costume." It looks a little like Sadie's lobster legs.

"Is it the lobster costume?"

"What lobster costume? Oh, no. Sadie is doing the lobster."

I sip my hot chocolate, nibble some muffin.

"So, whenever Amanda had bad dreams, she'd tell me about them. Want to tell me what's been keeping you up every night this week?"

"Not really," I mumble.

"You have every right to have bad dreams, Firefly. You … you survived. It's okay."

My chest is tight. My eyes tremble. I don't want to cry, not right now. I just want to go back to sleep.

Do I have to have these dreams forever, Aunt Gayle?

"You don't have to tell me, it's okay," my aunt says quietly. "But I think you should probably tell someone eventually. Maybe not that social worker in the bad eighties power suits, but someone. I can find someone for you to talk to, the school has told me they can help. The social worker could probably help find someone, too."

I take a deep breath. I hear the therapists at Jennie's. Take a breath. Breathe, Firefly. Take another breath, Firefly. Of course, they thought I was sixteen, everyone at Jennie's did. They didn't ask too many questions or demand ID at Jennie's, or no one would turn up for the free counseling.

Breathe, Firefly.

"I've been dreaming about …" I stop.

Start again.

"About getting caught last week. By the social worker. When it happened. And about Joanne. Calling for me. Taking a baseball bat to the cops." I look up, and my aunt raises her eyebrows.

"Yes, Sharlene Baker did mention the baseball bat. Sorry you had to see that."

"Well, she didn't like cops. Most of the time, I could calm her down. But I wasn't there." My voice starts to tremble. I look down at my hands. My voice gets that squeak to it that means I should probably stop trying to talk.

But I keep going.

"I would have gone home when she fell asleep, like usual. But I fell asleep in the park. I didn't mean to."

I have no idea what my aunt knows or doesn't know. I just have too many secrets here. I'm pretty sure Sharlene Baker would have told her that she found me in the park across the street from the house, in the company of a street person, during the scene that night with Joanne-the-mother.

But maybe not.

Tears. Oh yeah. Here they come. I pull the quilt over

my head. Tears pour down my cheeks in the stuffy darkness. My aunt is on her knees in front of me. She gently puts her hand on my knee.

"Firefly, it's not your job to take care of Joanne. She's the grownup. You're the kid. She's supposed to keep you safe. Not the other way around."

Then … well. Something kind of gives way in me. Part of me sobs under the quilt. I'm just wracked with sobs, while my kind aunt sits bravely at my feet, with her hand on my knee. It's awkward, but warm, her hand.

The other part of me is calm, distant, thinking *yeah, I've heard that before.* I heard that from the Jennie therapists, a few times. Moss Cart, too.

I'm the kid. I'm the one who's supposed to be taken care of.

But there wasn't anyone else to lead Joanne-the-mother through the darkness. Not any friends or co-workers to calm her down when she lost her job again and again — Joanne didn't have any. Not any family. Not even you, Aunt Gayle.

Only me.

I've been Joanne-the-mother's guiding light, flashing her toward safety since I was six. After my father left one night and didn't bother coming back. Or get in touch with us ever again.

Except for the night last week when she got arrested and I got caught by Sharlene Baker because I fell asleep on the park bench, I was the light in Joanne's dark world.

I've always been her Firefly in the dark.

THIRTEEN

Carrot

I wake up with rain pounding on the windows. Eventually Aunt Gayle led me to the bedroom, tucked me under the comforter on the floor. I did sleep, I think.

My eyes sting from dried tears.

Oh yeah, I cried. I cried under the comforter for quite a while until I fell asleep. And Aunt Gayle sat with me the whole time.

The rain pours down the windows. The clock says it's 11:07 a.m.

It's Saturday morning, the weekend before Halloween in a costume shop. I can hear people talking outside the apartment, lots of voices in the warehouse.

I get up, and Juggers looks up at me.

"You've been on the bed all night? You're almost as lazy as me, stray cat."

I tiptoe out into the apartment hallway. Aunt Gayle's door is open, her bed is made. She must be downstairs renting costumes to people for Halloween. Since it's the last Saturday before Halloween, I guess all the parties will be tonight.

"Oh, a Dickens flower girl!" I hear a girl squeal with excitement, she's standing just outside the apartment door. She must be looking at the Dickensian Rolling Judy that freaks me out so much. Even though the door is closed, I can hear her perfectly. It's creepy, a bit.

I sneak over and make sure the apartment door is locked (it wasn't), then I take a bath.

I don't care how many people are out there wandering around picking costumes for Halloween, I am not going to miss the chance to take a bath.

The lavender soap I used the first day, exactly one week ago today, is just a sliver in my hand.

I get dressed in those carefully ripped jeans again (pretty soon they'll be a laundry item, I realize that, but they're not laundry yet), and a Pink Floyd T-shirt from the clean pile. No idea what Pink Floyd is, but the T-shirt has a cool prism on it.

I open the apartment door, and I almost want to close it again.

Almost.

The warehouse is full of people. I mean, there are heads bopping among the racks of costumes as far as I can see.

I take a breath (*Breathe, Firefly*), close the apartment door behind me, and startle a girl standing next to the military coats rack.

"Oh, excuse me!" she squeals. Then she takes a longer look at me. "Um, do you work here?"

I shrug. "Not really, but I might be able to help you."

The girl sees an opportunity. "Well, do you know where the barmaid dresses are? Like something kind of old fashioned, but not too formal?"

I laugh a little. "Surprisingly, I do." Then I lead her to the "Saloon, Party Dress" row of costumes and show her where the shelves are for the saloon girl accessories and boots.

"Do you know how the pricing here works?" one man asks as soon as I've finished with Saloon Girl. He's holding what looks like a snake's head mask and a long, slithery green suit. I shake my head. "I'm sorry, I don't really work here, so no I don't. You'll have to ask downstairs at the cash register."

I get swamped then, since about five more people swarm around me. I lead two huge guys to the "Medieval" section, and they're delighted. They've got to be in their thirties, but they both start giggling and grab the knitted, chain mail leggings and fake leather chest plates. They start swinging the stage swords and shields at each other like little kids.

Geesh, people really do like dressing up.

But having dressed up myself a little lately, I get it.

I smile politely and walk away, but before I get very far another woman wants to know if we have any "Bride of Frankenstein" costumes. I show her the "Bride" section (there are literally five hundred wedding dresses there, from medieval times to futuristic robot bride), but she's on her own about the Frankenstein part, because I don't know.

The last person wants to know if there are any *vegetable* costumes.

I look at this person carefully. He's a teenager, I vaguely recognize him maybe.

"*Vegetable* costumes? Like ... carrots? Pumpkins? Pea pods? Edible vegetables kind of thing?" He laughs and nods, and I say, "Okay, we do. Come with me," and I lead him down the stairs to the main floor, where the Halloween frenzy is truly underway.

The main floor is just hopping. Sadie rushes past with armloads of clothes. She shouts, "Hi, Firefly!" as she heads back to the change rooms, where a bunch of people are waiting for their Halloween costumes.

Someone is playing the piano, and I recognize Ambrose, the actor. He's still wearing the black top hat. There are a few people standing around him, who also appear to be actors, or what I would imagine actors might look like, anyway: attractive and commanding. He notices me and waves, and says, "Bonjour, Mademoiselle Firefly!" with a flourish of his hat and a deep, beautiful voice.

I wave, nod, smile. "Hi, Ambrose," I say.

Nearby, Gillian and Stuart (possibly), the Ryerson students, are writing requests down from a small group of people. I guess Aunt Gayle asked them to come in today — the shop IS really busy. They both look kind of overworked. Then they lead the group over to the "Band Costumes/Musician" racks, where people start pawing through majorette costumes. A box filled with pom-poms and batons gets pulled off a shelf, and suddenly everyone is a majorette.

Aunt Gayle and Sylvia are both at the cash register, scanning clothes and bagging them in big cloth bags. There's a lineup almost out the door.

Edward is at the front door, counting people. He seems to be letting them in groups of five or so, as people leave.

I stand for a moment with my mouth open.

People are trying clothes on all over the warehouse, and plenty aren't even bothering with the change rooms. There are partially dressed people trying on police uniforms and sailor outfits, and three women are laughing hysterically. I mean, these ladies are peeing themselves laughing.

Then I see why. One of them has actually dressed in a costume, and she comes waddling out of the change room toward us.

She's a *lobster*.

There is just nothing as hilarious as a lobster costume. Sadie's beautiful claws stick way up above the lady's head, and her face grins from the red foam head with antennae waving around, six legs stick out of the foam body at the sides. A grade seven science project on lobsters rings a "lobsters actually have ten legs, eight legs at the sides and two large claws at the front" bell, but I'm probably the only person who notices or cares. We can't help it, everyone who sees her shuffling toward us, we all just laugh, including the kid with a thing for vegetables.

"Gloria! You are HILARIOUS!" one of the ladies laughs, then they all grab a lobster costume. One of them sees me watching and says, "We're a vocal quartet!" I just cannot imagine what kind of party they are going to dressed as four singing lobsters. It takes a certain self-confidence to go to a Halloween party dressed as one quarter of a lobster quartet.

This idea actually makes me quite happy. I'm perilously close to giggling.

I lead the teenager to the "Novelty Halloween Costumes" rack, which is frankly looking pretty picked-over at this point, and it's not even noon.

I dig around, and there it is, the carrot costume that the TVO show used. I grab it and the bag attached.

"Will a carrot do?" I shove the huge, orange, foam shape at him, and he grins.

"Thanks, Firefly," he says, kind of shyly.

"Wait, do I know you?"

"Yeah, I sit with you in French, and I'm in your Library support group. It's Charlie. I liked your flyboy costume last week." I look more closely, and I do kind of recognize him.

"Oh yeah. Sorry. I'm not that great with faces. And you're kind of out of context, not in school. Come on," I say, and lead him through a group of people lining up for the "Ghosts/Ghouls" rack.

There are too many people in here.

I make our way to the cash register, and Aunt Gayle notices me.

"Firefly!" she calls, then comes around the counter and sees Charlie clutching the carrot costume.

"Morning, Aunt Gayle. This is Charlie. He's in my French class; library too. He wants to rent this carrot. Is that okay?"

Now there's something you don't say every day.

This is Charlie. He wants to rent this carrot.

Not even Moss Cart could have come up with something that bizarre. I'm kind of enjoying this, I must admit.

Aunt Gayle beams. She shakes Charlie's hand.

"Hi Charlie. Of course. A special deal for a friend of Firefly's. We're so busy today, what's a carrot between friends? It's on the house." Then she turns to me. "I made bacon and eggs with sausages. There's some left in the kitchen in the oven. Toast, too. Soon we're getting pizza for lunch, though. Do you want to stay for lunch, Charlie? You must be starving, Firefly."

Wow, Aunt Gayle. Just casually invite the weird kid with a penchant for vegetables for lunch.

"Sure, thanks," Charlie says. He frankly seems a little bedazzled.

Then I lead him toward the kitchen, just as the singing lobster ladies leave the shop with their lobster costumes in big bags. There's not a lot of room, and we wait patiently as the claws, antennae, and red foam bodies squeeze past us and out the door. Edward lets five more people in the front door; he's holding a counting clicker in his hands. Click, click, click, and I peek past him out the door. There's a lineup down the street. People are standing under umbrellas in the rain, patiently waiting for their Halloween dreams to come true.

"Hi, Firefly," Edward says happily.

I smile, say hello back, lead Charlie into the kitchen.

Shut the kitchen door, and it's suddenly blessedly quiet.

"Wow, weird place you live," Charlie says. He places the foam carrot costume and the bag in the corner of the kitchen. The carrot is going to fit over his head and go down to his thighs, there's a place cut out for his face, and there are green leaves above. There's an orange long-sleeved shirt and orange tights to cover his legs in the bag, orange gloves, and what look like soft orange shoe covers.

I may have to insist that Charlie model this for me at some point.

"Yeah, I guess it is kind of weird. But it's Halloween. I honestly have no idea what it's like the rest of the time, since I just moved in. Maybe it's just quiet and creepy the rest of the year."

"I doubt it," he says. "Your aunt seems too fun for it to be creepy and quiet in here."

I pour myself a coffee, offer him one, which he accepts. I open the oven door, and the smell of warm food makes my stomach growl. I wear the oven mitts, take out the bowls of scrambled eggs, bacon, sausages, and a plate of warm toast and put it all on the kitchen table. The oven mitts are red, and for a moment I think that other kids would have to make do with red oven mitts as lobster claws, if they wanted to go out for Halloween as a lobster.

Not me, though. Although I suddenly wonder, with a pang, if the lobster costumes will be back from their singing party in time for me to wear one on Halloween next Wednesday.

I get down plates, pull cutlery out of the drawer. I put glasses on the table, get the orange juice carton out of the fridge. I haven't done any of these things in such a long time. Joanne-the-mother didn't exactly keep a well-stocked fridge. Or a clean kitchen. Or anything on the shelves.

Not since she lost her cashier job.

We sit. We eat. We chat about school. Charlie is nice, and actually quite funny.

And part of me is thinking, wow, Firefly, just look how normal you are. Food, plates, cutlery, more food than two people can eat, all in one place. No Joanne-the-mother screaming for water or food, or help going to the bathroom. Or for you.

If there weren't singing lobster quartets, medieval warriors, and baton-swinging majorettes outside the kitchen door, you could be totally mistaken for just another normal teenager.

So normal, no one would suspect a thing.

FOURTEEN

There's Always a Guy
in a Gorilla Suit

After Charlie leaves, I spend the rest of Saturday helping in the shop, and it's busy. Aunt Gayle says the store will stay open until 8 p.m. and it's been fun watching people get dressed for a Halloween party.

After a while, though, people get a little desperate. Around 7 p.m., Aunt Gayle tells Edward to stop the line from getting any longer, and there are still twenty people waiting outside in the rain. So she lets them all in, but no one else.

And I help people find police uniforms, Dracula costumes (which I personally think are a Halloween fail if you've gone to the trouble to go to a costume shop with seven million pieces in it) and a lot more. There are four twenty-somethings who choose sixties clothes, like those pants Aunt Gayle was working on for the Summer of Love, 1967. Long wigs, long striped pants with vests, flowery shirts with long leather boots, chains, and peace-sign necklaces.

They really do look great. Aunt Gayle takes their photo, and Sadie posts it on The Corseted Lady Instagram account.

When the last customer leaves around 9:15, Aunt Gayle orders a huge feast of Indian food, and we all collapse onto the couches and in the kitchen to devour it. I'm starving.

Once I eat, I take another bath (maybe I should keep it to one a day soon), then Aunt Gayle and I watch the first episode of a British show called *Downton Abbey* on Netflix. Aunt Gayle says she loves it, mostly because of the period costumes.

I just can't believe people ever lived like that, in castles with servants.

I couldn't think of a more different existence from my life with Joanne-the-mother.

On Sunday, The Corseted Lady is much quieter, although Aunt Gayle opens the store, in case anyone wants to return or rent anything.

I get up late. My sleeping arrangement has now settled into a regular thing: me on the floor and Juggers on the bed. This morning though, interestingly, I don't wake up with a terrible dream. I don't think I dream in the night, either.

Probably just too tired to dream after working all day, but I'll take it.

I get dressed in a clean pair of purple track pants. They say "Queen's" across the butt, and I put on the Pink Floyd T-shirt again. I like it, but I can tell it's barely socially acceptable after twenty-four hours wearing it. My pits stink a little. Nothing like they have stunk in previous months; now that I can access laundry and hot baths whenever I want, I don't actually have to stink.

Stinkiness is a choice, at least at the moment.

I take off the shirt. I put on a plain light blue shirt with a Nike swoosh over the heart.

Then I drift downstairs for breakfast just as Aunt Gayle is opening the front door at 11:00 a.m.

There's a guy dressed in a gorilla suit standing there.

I stop. How often do you see a guy in a gorilla suit at your front door? I mean, maybe it happens now and then. It's just never happened to me.

Aunt Gayle turns to me and says, "There's always a guy in a gorilla suit, Firefly." I snort. "Things You Learn Living in a Costume Shop," she adds. I grin. Okay, Aunt Gayle.

Gorilla Guy has got red running shoes on, and a red polka dot tie, and a little fedora perched on his gorilla head. He's got a cigar in his hand.

"No smoking in the gorilla suit," Aunt Gayle snaps.

Wow, Aunt Gayle, what a hypocrite!

But then she says, "It's really flammable. Do you want to burn yourself beyond recognition?" Then I get it. Sure, it's probably a tinder box of a costume.

Gorilla Guy drops the cigar on the wet sidewalk, then shuffles into the store. He plonks himself onto one of the overstuffed couches and opens one of the magazines. If he starts playing the piano, I'm going to be undone.

I wander into the kitchen.

Aunt Gayle is making coffee for the customers. She has a big stainless steel coffee pot, and little paper cups and creamers and stuff, on a table by the door.

She makes a coffee, storms over to Gorilla Guy on the couch, hands it to him.

"Drink this, then get changed and go, please," she demands. "Halloween party's over."

I watch from the kitchen, mesmerized. Now Gorilla Guy is reading a magazine and sipping coffee. Aunt Gayle breezes past me back into the kitchen, and says, "You can't let them get too comfortable. Especially the ones still dressed up after the party's over the next day."

I grin. It's pretty funny.

Gorilla Guy is totally happy. Once he finishes his coffee, he goes into a change room, then comes out in his ordinary, drab clothes. He could be an accountant or something, just a normal guy.

He returns with his gorilla costume, holding it lovingly like he's going to miss it. Drops it politely on the counter and leaves.

I think he'll be back next Halloween. I hope his dreams were fulfilled for another year.

People trickle in and out of the shop, a few to return costumes, a few to rent things, but no one else still in costume.

Then around three o'clock, a trio of clowns turn up.

They're still drunk and possibly high from last night's party.

Which makes me uneasy. I edge toward the stairs.

They're rowdy and loud. One guy keeps singing, "Baby, you ain't seen nothing yet!" at the top of his lungs. He seems the drunkest, and his friends keep telling him to "SHUT UP, BILL!"

I'll take the calm, magazine-reading, coffee-sipping Gorilla Guy who could have played piano but thankfully didn't, over these people.

I watch the clowns, keep my distance. They seem to have the impression there's still a Halloween party going on. Aunt Gayle will have none of it, and orders them around like a sergeant major. These guys don't even get an offer of coffee. Luckily Sadie comes into the store a few minutes later and helps Aunt Gayle manage the out-of-control clowns.

I've seen enough drunk and high people in my life.

Joanne-the-mother partied with a lot of interesting friends for a while there right after my father left. They'd even turn up again now and then years later, whenever she had a job. And money. They think they're charming, or funny, or really smart. They're not. Not any of those things, at least not when they're out of control. I've seen people screaming at the top of their lungs in the night, tearing their clothes off, staggering in front of cars, bellowing at the stars, at the air.

At me.

At least they give you enough warning to steer clear. Most of the time.

But what you really have to watch out for?

When they're hiding it, and doing a good job too, so you can't tell if they are or if they aren't drunk or high or whatever until it's too late. Puzzling until you figure it out at age six.

Mom, I'm hungry.

Slapslapslap.

Get an apple. Shussshhhup.

With Moss Cart, though, no matter how wild he was, I could always calm him. For some reason, he was never scary.

I slide up the stairs, vanish into the apartment, until I hear Aunt Gayle and Sadie get the clowns back into their street clothes and out the door. Those two are tough.

They have taken absolutely *no* crap from the clowns.

I hear a man's voice too at one point, so maybe Max has come in from the van to help. I can hear him calmly say, "No, you're not doing that. Get your clown shoes off," and more in a deep, rumbly voice.

I lie on the bedroom floor in my nest and Juggers actually comes and sits at my feet, watching me. We study each other as the clowns make a fuss in the shop below.

"They're drunk," I say out loud, and the cat closes his eyes for a moment. It's started raining outside again, and rain hits the window in noisy splatters.

"Or high, maybe. I don't like it." The cat closes his eyes, then crouches at my feet. I honestly think he's purring. He's almost touching my foot.

Almost.

"Aren't you supposed to sleep on the bed?" I ask, and he loses interest in me then, and marches out of the room. Touchy cat.

As soon as I hear the door shut behind the scary clowns, I head back down to the shop.

For the rest of the afternoon, more costumes get returned, but mostly the customers have bagged them and return them politely.

No more loud, obnoxious, out of control customers.

A few costumes get rented too, and I help a mother and daughter find a "Little Bo Peep and sheep" costume. The mother is the shepherdess and the daughter is supposed to be the sheep.

Which is frankly quite weird and gives me the creeps. I get the feeling the little girl does *not* want to be a sheep. She has her arms crossed, staring out into the warehouse.

Her mother comes out of a change room into the shop, wearing the big blue hoop skirt and the bonnet and the shepherd's staff and everything, and the little girl says flat out, "You look ridiculous."

But her mother just laughs. She says, "No, we're adorable! Where's your sheep costume?"

I show the kid the lamb outfit. It's white and puffy, with little black ears. The girl is about nine and looks at me with such woe in her eyes. Her mother has gone back to the change room, and the little girl says, "I do NOT want to wear that."

I look down at her. I nod. "I guess I wouldn't want to either. Not at your age. But these days I wear all kinds of costumes." The little girl looks quizzical. But she's listening.

"Really?"

I nod. "Yeah. Really. I went to school all last week in different costumes. I was a flyboy, a saloon girl, a monk. I was even a medieval warrior, and you know what?"

She shrugs. "What?"

"No one even cared. I'm not kidding. No one even noticed. You live in a big city. You can wear whatever you want. It's fine. And who doesn't like lambs? I mean, sure, there are definitely cooler costumes in here, maybe you could ask your mother for one of those next year?"

She considers this, then takes the lamb suit out of my hand. Her mother calls from the change room, and she rolls her eyes. But she kind of smiles, too, and I think, *Not bad, Firefly. Helping the next generation manage the parental weirdness. Not bad.*

She's so cute when she reappears in the lamb costume, that I have to force myself to remain solemn. She stops in front of me, all puffy white lambiness, and says sternly, "What cooler costumes? Like, a for-instance?"

"There are seven million costumes in here. You can be pretty much anything. Do you like Mario Brothers? Batman? Mermaids? Construction dude? Giant pea pod? Lobsters?"

When I say "lobsters," she raises her eyebrows. Her mother breezes by with the Little Bo Peep costume, and calls her on her way to the counter to pay Aunt Gayle for the rentals.

The little girl waves me down and I bend over, ear to her mouth.

"Next year, lobster or possibly medical warrior," she whispers.

"I think you mean 'medieval' warrior, but there are medical warriors too. And good choices. Very powerful," I nod. Then with all the grace she can manage, the little lamb turns and follows her mother out the door.

You go be fierce, little lamb. Go kick butt out in the world.

And also, go be the most adorable lamb ever.

Because you can definitely be both.

FIFTEEN

Boy Two

bang my hands on the cop car window.

Let her go! Please, just let her go! I can talk to her! BANGBANGBANG! JOANNE! I slap my hands on the window harder, call Joanne's name again, but the cruiser pulls away with the siren flashing, redblueredblue.

"Your mom will be okay, Fifi. I'm here to take care of you."

I wake up. Sweat pours off me.

It's Sharlene Baker's voice in my head. What a crap voice to wake up to.

My heart hammers in my chest. I gasp, trying to catch my breath. The sun pours through the window onto the bed.

Aunt Gayle knocks on the door. "Firefly? Monday morning, yay."

Juggers raises his head off the bed, the sun shines

through his tattered ears and turns them kitten pink.

"Okay," I call. I roll over back into my nest, wait until my heart stops hammering. Do I have to get up? Really? Is anyone going to care if I make it to Math, and French, and Music today? Maybe History too — I can't remember what classes I have.

Does it matter?

And can I please stop dreaming about Joanne-the-mother?

But I do get up. I eye Juggers as I stagger past the bed, and he's lying in a patch of sunlight. He stretches out all four paws, yawns, regards me.

"Seriously lazy, you," I mutter at him, but continue into the bathroom.

I take a quick shower. Then I choose a pair of black, stovepipe jeans from the pile of clean laundry from Aunt Gayle, and a black T-shirt with huge red lips and tongue on it. No idea what this is, but it's weird and I like it.

And today … I'm a cop.

This is one of Aunt Gayle's largest sections, the police uniforms. She was one of the first costume designers on a series of funny movies about a police force, and she must have over one thousand cop costumes, all different kinds. The racks just go on and on.

I choose a leather jacket. Big, shiny black helmet. Green goggles, the big leather gloves, the heavy-duty leather boots.

Behold! *Firefly, motorcycle cop.*

I eat breakfast with Aunt Gayle (Cheerios, toast and blueberry jam, orange juice, coffee), say hello to Sadie and Max, who are walking back to the shop with two coffees, then head off to school. Queen Street is busy with people doing ordinary daytime things: well-dressed office workers get on the streetcar, kids go to schools with parents, lots of people head to the coffee shops on every corner, a man sits with an empty Tim Hortons cup in front of the liquor store. A sign beside him says, "Whatever you got helps! Have a nice day!"

I drop a few coins into the guy's cup courtesy of Aunt Gayle. He nods at me.

Get a sub, buddy, I think. *Sub sandwiches are the cheapest and most filling for the money. A sub can hold you a whole day.*

But he probably knows that.

The motorcycle cop goggles are green-tinted. Frankly, the world looks a lot better green.

I get to school, get my math book from my locker, wander halls, get to class.

Normal, normal, normal.

Math class breezes by, and amazingly, math is starting to come back to me. I walk the halls of Leslie Street Central with my green-tinted goggles, and honestly, no one seems to notice me.

Then, I slide into the desk beside Charlie in French class.

"What are you today?" he asks as I sit down.

"Motorcycle cop, obviously," I say. The other two girls at our desk of four come and sit, and they tell me their names: Charlotte and Leah.

"What are you going to be on Halloween?" Charlie asks me.

"Lobster."

Charlotte and Leah are about to say something to me, when Madame Frances comes to our desks with a task: we are supposed to talk to each other as though we are meeting at a coffee shop.

Madame Frances has given each group of four a set of booklets, for whatever their task might be. (The group of four next to us are struggling through a terrifying-sounding buying-a-dress-for-the-prom scenario, so the coffee shop option is seriously okay.)

But for our coffee-shop scenario, there are only three books. Madame Frances hands out one to Charlie, one to Charlotte, one to Leah, then stops in front of me.

"Firefly, I'm so sorry! I don't have a booklet for you!" She seems distressed, and Madame Frances is nothing if not earnest and sweet. French matters in here.

I smile at her through the cop goggles. (Madame Frances looks great in green.)

"No worries at all, Madame Frances. I can play along. I've spent plenty of time in coffee shops."

She nods, then promises to look for the missing booklet.

She heads away, back to her desk, where she does seem to be looking for something with a manic intensity.

The booklet starts with Girl One: Charlotte.

Girl One: "Bonjour, copains! Vous aimez du café?"

("Hello, buddies! Would you like coffee?")

She manages to put such life and effort into this statement, that Leah, Charlie, and I raise our eyebrows.

"Way too much for Monday, Char," Leah says. Madame Frances looks over (she's still fussing for the lost booklet, now she's nearby in a supply closet) and calls, "En français, s'il vous plaît!"

Boy One/Charlie: "Oui, j'aimerais du café, merci!"

("Yes, I would love a coffee, thank you!")

Charlie manages to make these words sound like anything but French.

Girl Two/Leah (who sighs enormously, she's wearing a huge amount of mascara, which looks amazing on her, I suspect she's got a lot going on emotionally): "Oui, moi aussi. J'aime du café avec du lait et sucre."

("Oh yes, me too. I love coffee with milk and sugar.")

Now the booklet says, Boy Two (although I have no booklet to read from), and Leah slides hers across the table to me to read, but I push it politely back to her. No book? Then I'm free to go off book, as far as I see it.

I say: "Oui, j'aime du café. Le Tim Hortons a des toilettes trés propres et c'est ouvertes à toutes heures. C'est nécessaire quand tu habites quelque fois dans un parc."

Charlie looks at me, but Charlotte and Leah don't respond. My French isn't actually that bad, although I'm hardly bilingual.

"I did extended French in middle school," I say casually.

"What did you just say?" Leah whispers in English, darting a look at Madame Frances. "What was that about the bathrooms at Tim Hortons?"

"It's clean and open all hours," Charlie whispers. "Which is necessary," he adds, then stops. I smile, nod.

The banality continues.

Girl One and Girl Two order coffees and croissants for Boys One and Two (Charlie keeps muttering how binary and sexist this is), and Boy One and Two are supposed to talk about soccer while they're waiting for the girls to bring food and coffee.

But Boy Two keeps going off book, since she doesn't have one.

In the cop outfit, behind the heavy green goggles and under the helmet and the leather jacket, I can just say anything, be anyone.

I guess a costume will do that for you.

My French copains at the coffee shop get to hear a lot about my life. Boy Two just keeps feeding out little pieces of information among the banal chatter about croissants and summer holidays.

Little gems like, "C'est délicieuse. Et oui, j'ai faim. Je n'ai pas mangé aujourd'hui."

And, "Si tu bois trés lentement, tu peux rester à Tim Hortons tout le jour."

Girls One and Two listen but don't respond. Those girls are hardened to life's woes? Or maybe their French is just really terrible?

But Boy One, poor Boy One. By the time French class is over, he's got tears in his eyes.

I leave the classroom when the bell rings, and I hear Charlie behind me.

"Firefly! Firefly, wait!" He runs after me down the hall.

I stop in front of my locker, where he catches up with me. We both stare at my locker, which has an interesting addition to it. Someone has scrawled across it, in black chalk: FIREFLY FREAK.

I swipe at it with my cop gloves. It comes off, but Charlie grabs my hand.

"Stop! You need to show someone! Take a picture at least."

"With what?"

"Your cellphone?" Charlie holds up his phone.

"I don't have one," I say. It's true. I've never had one, there just wasn't ever any money for one for me. Aunt Gayle has already told me she'll get me a phone as soon as she has time. I'm honestly not that interested. What's all the fuss about? I've made it this far without one.

I guffaw, and rub the rest of the message off my locker, but Charlie takes a picture before I get it all wiped off.

I hope the leather motorcycle cop gloves come clean. It does seem to be black chalk, so no big deal, probably.

Charlie watches, resigned.

"You shouldn't have erased it," he says, glum.

"Come on Charlie, like I care what some stupid high school student thinks of me." I open my locker, grab my backpack and books, then head out of the school, toward Queen Street. It's lunch time, and I'm starving. He hesitates, watches me leave.

"Firefly!" he calls, then catches up with me. I stop in front of the coffee shop at the corner. Wow, coffee shops *are* everywhere.

"Firefly," he says. He's been running and he's not even winded. "Look, stop. I'm sorry ... I ... uh ... I guess those things you said in French class. About Tim Hortons?" He's stuck. He doesn't know how to go any further. He wants to ask if they're true, I think, but can't.

I stand still. The world is so green behind these goggles.

Green kids walk past. A green dog. Green lady walking her dog. Green streetcar. Green kid running past without a shirt.

Skinny Kid runs past us on the sidewalk. His pale green chest is ... shirtless.

Not-So-Skinny Kid is close behind him, running fast.

Then everything happens in green slow motion. Any other day, I may not have done this, but the green filter on the world, the powerful motorcycle costume.

The huge leather cop boots.

Boy Two telling it like it is.

I can be anyone.

My foot, in its big motorcycle cop leather boot, lazily extends itself across the sidewalk. The boot goes out, just far enough, it's completely in charge here, not me …

… and Not-So-Skinny Kid goes flying over it.

It's a solid boot. I barely feel him trip over my foot encased inside.

And then in a green ball of fury, Not-So-Skinny Kid rolls and rolls and rolls to a stop on the sidewalk. He lies in front of the Shoppers Drug Mart for a second.

Dazed.

Then he gets up and stares at me and Charlie. Skinny Kid keeps running down Queen Street and escapes. He doesn't even look back.

Funny. Not-So-Skinny Kid is the only one who doesn't look so great in green.

Not-So-Skinny Kid gets up, comes toward us. He's going to punch me? And me, in a motorcycle cop outfit.

He's going to hurt his hand if he punches me in the head, I think. Maybe I should warn him? This is a movie-grade costume helmet, buddy! You're going to get hurt!

Charlie has frozen like a statue. He's just staring at Not-So-Skinny Kid, who continues toward us.

I think about that scene in the movie *A Christmas Story* (one of the few movies I DO know about because

I watched it whenever I could if we had electricity and a working television), when Ralphie finally loses it and gives it to Scut Farkus, with both barrels ...

... but nothing nearly as dramatic or interesting happens.

Not-So-Skinny Kid closes in. People move out of his way on the sidewalk because he's coming toward us like a pit bull, and I open my mouth and say ...

"You're really a huge jerk, chasing that skinny kid every day like that."

I mean, I just don't know when to shut up, obviously.

And he stands in front of Charlie and me, and he's heaving he's so mad. He's about to hit me (he balls up his fist, and he *is* going to hit me on the motorcycle cop helmet) when ...

... BEEP! BEEP!

A sensible, blue, four-door sedan pulls over to the curb beside me, and the passenger door flings open. Sharlene Baker sticks her head over the seat and says, "Hey, Norman! And ... Firefly! Is that you? I'm going to see your aunt. Do you want a ride?"

Norman? Really?

Interesting dilemma, though.

Get in the car with Sharlene Shoulder-Pads Baker?

Or stand and get pummeled by *Norman*? (And possibly hear his hand break on the helmet.)

"Come on, Charlie," I say, and we both jump into the

social worker's car, slam doors.

I sit beside Sharlene Baker in the front seat, and as we drive away, I can't help it.

I give Norman-Not-So-Skinny Kid that not-fit-for-polite-company gesture I used the first time I met him. That's twice in one week. Which is not like me at all. I blame the costume.

But what's a Firefly in a motorcycle cop costume to do?

SIXTEEN

Rriiiiip!

Charlie and I are eating bagels with cream cheese and lox in the kitchen at The Corseted Lady.

Sharlene Baker is sitting across the kitchen table. She has just told me that Joanne-the-mother is doing well in addiction counseling at CAMH.

What she actually says is, "Your mother is responding well to treatment at the Queen Street addiction facility." When I don't respond, or look at her, she says more.

"She'd like to see you, Firefly, when she's allowed visitors. She's still in isolation, plus she might be facing charges for the baseball bat incident. It's going to take a while," Sharlene Baker says.

"Lockdown," Aunt Gayle adds.

They both look at me, and I just shrug.

Then Sharlene Baker reaches into her bulging, open

briefcase and hands me a sealed, white envelope.

"*Fifi*" is scrawled across the front in big, loopy, child-ish handwriting. It's from Joanne-the-mother. I take the envelope, place it face-down beside my plate, don't look at it again. Chew my bagel, look out the window.

Tree. Lamppost. Top of building. CN Tower.

Aunt Gayle chews her thumbnail, looks at me, clearly needs a cigarette.

She still won't light up in front of Sharlene Baker, but there's no way the social worker doesn't know that Aunt Gayle is a smoker. The whole place reeks of smoke.

There are bigger issues than smoking maybe, for Sharlene Baker.

Charlie has stayed quiet, and solemn. He eyes the enve-lope beside my plate, though.

Sharlene Baker turns to me.

"I called earlier this morning, and your Aunt said I could drop by with the envelope at noon. And I was sur-prised to see you talking to Norman Jakes on the street." She looks at me expectantly.

I shrug, chew, swallow bagel. "I don't know him. I didn't know his name until you just told me."

Sharlene Baker sits a little straighter. Her shoulder pads look a little perkier.

"Oh. I see."

"He's bullying some poor kid, though," I add. "Tears his shirt off him every day." *Let's see you social work your way out of that one*, I think. But Sharlene Baker nods and sighs.

"I'm not surprised," she says.

"His name is Scott Durkin," Charlie pipes up, and everyone looks at him like we forgot he was there. "The kid who Norman bullies. It's Scott Durkin," Charlie affirms, quietly.

Sharlene Baker nods again and says, "I see," once more. She looks at the ceiling, takes a deep breath, takes a moment to consider Norman Jakes and Scott Durkin. She seems familiar with them.

"They're stepbrothers. Complicated family," she says. Then she gets up and tries to snap her briefcase closed, but it's too bulging to close properly, so she picks it up and hugs it to her chest.

"I have to go — I'm late for a meeting with the city about shelter beds for street kids — but I can arrange a meeting with you and your mother, Firefly, when she's allowed a visitor, if you like. See you on Wednesday, we can talk about it then." Then Sharlene Baker and her gigantic shoulder pads stomp out the kitchen and out the front door.

The little bell tinkles as she leaves.

Aunt Gayle has already lit up and inhales her cigarette deeply. Charlie and I stand up. He seems embarrassed, but I guess he's just been part of something kind of private. He heard a social worker talk about my mother in isolation, in treatment, maybe with a court case pending. He just saw that same social worker hand me a letter from my mother, and really, other than a few hints today in French class, he doesn't know the first thing about me. Or didn't.

Other than I want to be a lobster for Halloween.

We rise to leave the kitchen and Aunt Gayle says, "Firefly, do you ..." She points at the envelope on the table and starts again. "Do you want me to read that first?" She darts a look at Charlie, who looks woeful.

I consider the envelope for a moment.

What could Joanne-the-mother say to me in that letter that she hasn't said hundreds of times before? Now she's straightening up and remorseful? Sorry, Fifi? I screwed up, Fifi? I shouldn't have gone after that cop with a baseball bat, Fifi?

I love you, I'll try to be a better mother, Fifi?

Sorry for your crappy childhood?

I pick up the sealed envelope, and before I can stop myself, I tear it in half.

Rrriiiiip!

What a satisfying sound ripped paper is when you need one.

Then I walk over to the garbage can, pop the lid with the foot pedal, and drop the two pieces of the envelope inside.

"No thanks, Aunt Gayle, but thanks for asking," I say.

"Come on, Charlie," I add, and Charlie and I leave the kitchen. A few clients are out at the returns counter, and Sadie is taking care of them. The place is full today. A few more customers are here to rent costumes for Halloween on Wednesday, but it's nothing like Saturday. No hordes of people.

Edward walks past with a ladder and says hello. I wave to Sylvia, who is sewing madly in the sewing room.

BRRRRR, BRRRRR, BRRRRR.

She sees me, smiles and waves, then politely closes the sewing room door.

I take a quick look at the returns, but there aren't any lobster costumes there. The lobsters are still out singing somewhere, I guess.

I take off my motorcycle cop costume, the leather coat, the helmet, the boots and put it all on the "returns" rack to clean later, then I take Charlie to the apartment.

"Cool place," he says, looking around. The afternoon sun is just peeking through the windows at the west side of the apartment, and it does look cool. Cozy, even. The city is all stainless-steel gray and frosted blue glass off to the west.

We settle in the living room. I lie down on the couch and pull the quilt over me. Charlie takes the chair.

"Nice apartment," he says again, then contents himself with silence.

He's good at being quiet. He doesn't mention the letter.

We sit, and I don't speak. Juggers jumps up onto the couch and settles at the very far end. He looks at Charlie but doesn't flee. Eventually Charlie says, "I guess you and your mother have a tough relationship?" His voice goes up at the end of the question, along with his eyebrows.

I nod. "Oh yeah, you could say that. Tough is barely the beginning."

He looks at me. "Okay, well, you can tell me or not. But you can, if you want. Anytime." He looks at his cellphone. "We have to go. School starts in ten minutes." He stands up, and I don't move.

"You go on without me. I'll see you tomorrow."

"Okay." He hesitates beside me, like he wants to say more. But I cover myself with the quilt up to the chin, and he looks at me and Juggers; a girl and her beloved cat all curled up and cozy on the sunny couch.

We're not going anywhere.

Maybe never again.

"Well, bye. See you tomorrow then. Thanks for lunch."

Then he leaves the apartment, and I hear him clomping down the stairs. He says "Bye!" to someone, probably Sadie, then I hear the shop bell tinkle.

Charlie's gone.

Sharlene Baker is gone.

Joanne-the-mother is gone.

And Firefly Warren is gone, gone, gone, too.

SEVENTEEN

EIGHTEEN

Fugue

I lose twelve hours.

I stay on the couch, under the quilt, for twelve hours in a dark, unseeing, unmoving, disconnected void. I know that now, because it's the next day, and I finally crawled out from the dark place.

I cried, I know that much.

I could hear, in a way. I could see, too (through the constant stream from my eyes). I could even move and roll over. I was breathing, I was alive. But I was stuck somewhere, somewhere empty and black, that I couldn't come back from. Floating, disembodied, nothing.

What did I hear? What did I see? What did I feel for those twelve hours?

Aunt Gayle's voice: "I called the school and said you wouldn't be back this afternoon."

A plate of muffins and a pot of tea appear on the table before me.

Sunshine on my face.

Sunshine on Juggers (he stretches and rolls over).

Sun passes over the chair.

Sun splashes the far wall.

No sun.

Later a bowl of chili appears before me.

Later still, Aunt Gayle says, "I read it. The letter. I pulled it out of the garbage, I hope you don't mind. Let's just say it's nothing new in there. And I'll go see her, Firefly. You don't have to. I'll do it. Just so you know."

Then nothing.

Nothing.

Nothing.

Nothing.

Nothing, for a long while.

Until the sun comes up, and Aunt Gayle asks me a question, and I answer.

Firefly, what do you want for breakfast?

Cheerios.

That's it. I just wake up, say Cheerios, then get up from the couch. Which is weird, I know, and felt weird and sounds weird now. But I guess I was hungry?

I was stuck in the dark place, and then I wasn't.

I'm in the kitchen now, eating.

Here's what Aunt Gayle and Sadie tell me about the last twelve hours:

Juggers stayed with me on the couch until he slinked off at dawn.

Aunt Gayle stayed with me the whole time, too. And Sadie sat with me a few hours.

Around midnight, when I hadn't moved or spoken for hours but I didn't appear to be sleeping, just staring, they called Sharlene Baker, who put them through to a therapist for kids at CAMH — the Centre for Addiction and Mental Health.

I have a new therapist, starting Thursday.

On the advice of the therapist, they checked my breathing, talked to me, stayed with me. I rolled away, or shook my head, or frowned. Dissociative, but alive. I even got up to go to the bathroom once, which they took as a good sign.

Still in my body, at least partly.

So they talked to me. When I slowly started to answer and come back from the darkness, they gently talked more.

What do you want for breakfast, Firefly?

Cheerios.

Do you want some tea?

Yes, please.

I sit up.

I say: *I'm starving.*

Then: *I'm thirsty.*

Then after catching a whiff of myself: *I need a bath.*

And what I think is this: where have I been? How can it be *the next day*?

How can my aunt have prepared tea, muffins, and chili, made phone calls, worried about me, talked to a social worker and child therapist, and I didn't know?

I don't want this to happen again, whatever this is. Not ever.

I'm worried and sheepish. Embarrassed honestly. What just happened?

Sunshine pours in the kitchen window. It's a beautiful day outside. Blue sky, bright sunshine. I put down my spoon and put my hands in my lap. I look at Sadie.

"What really happened to me last night?"

Sadie puts down her sewing and looks over at Aunt Gayle, who is standing beside the fridge. They both look at me, and Sadie answers: "Well, the therapist said it's possibly a response to stress. PTSD. Dissociation. Maybe even a partial fugue state, but that's really quite rare."

I frown.

Okay, PTSD. I get that. Post-traumatic stress disorder. One of the therapists at Jennie's told me about that, symptoms and such. What to watch out for, dissociation, panic attacks, losing track of time and place, that kind of thing. But fugue state? Isn't a fugue a piece of music?

I didn't hear any music.

"A *fugue* state?" I ask this casually, take a sip of tea. But I'm scared. I know how it felt: dark, empty, nothing. I never want to feel that way again.

Sadie and Aunt Gayle look at each other, and Aunt Gayle leans toward me.

"The letter. Joanne's letter. Her handwriting. You didn't have any warning, and seeing it just brought everything back. Too much all at once. Or that's what the therapist suggested."

That makes sense. Seeing her wild handwriting was almost like having her in the room.

Aunt Gayle looks worried and sounds really sad.

"I'm so sorry, Firefly. I shouldn't have let Sharlene Baker bring you Joanne's letter without some warning. It wasn't fair to spring it on you like that. It won't happen again."

I take a deep breath. "I really don't want to talk about her for a while, okay?" Aunt Gayle and Sadie both nod. Aunt Gayle goes to make more tea, and Sadie looks down at her stitches. She's mending a torn coat seam on an eighteenth-century smoking jacket.

Joanne is out there. Alive. She is Joanne-the-mother. My mother. And I will have to deal with her, somehow, sometime.

We all know this.

But not today.

After breakfast, Aunt Gayle is all business, bustling

around the shop, angrily puffing cigarettes and stubbing them out in her glass ashtray. Then she goes into her office, and I don't see her again for a while.

I think maybe she's feeling guilty. Maybe managing her niece and her bat-wielding, addict sister is too much for her? I don't blame her. Until a few days ago, I wasn't her problem, she hadn't seen me in years. She barely knew I existed.

I suddenly feel like I really shouldn't be here, this is too much for everyone to deal with.

I'm too much to deal with.

It wouldn't be hard to get back to the park. And I have a key to the house. I know Joanne isn't there. I could talk to Moss Cart. Go to school from there …

… but that's the first place everyone would look if I went missing. The cops, the social worker, they all know where I live. Where Joanne-the-mother lives.

Where we lived.

I feel a little strangely dazed, and I get up and sit down a few times, until Sadie says quietly, "Maybe a bath would be nice? You don't have to do anything today, Firefly. In fact, the therapist said you should just rest."

I nod. A bath. She knows me well.

After I eat, drink some more tea (I'm starting to think maybe I should cut down on the coffee), wander around the shop (still no lobsters), I follow Sadie's advice and get into a warm bath. My toe sticks above the water line.

My toe is clean.

My toe is alive.

My toe is good.

Everyone at Jennie's always told me to try to love one thing about myself each day. Since there is nothing too repulsive about my toe at the moment, I guess I can start there.

It's not a perfect toe, far from it. But it deserves my respect. I've walked pretty far with that toe. Stubbed it on a lot of sidewalk. It deserves my friendship.

One day I may get to love it, although at the moment I don't see how.

The letter from Joanne-the-mother keeps popping into my head.

I can see her handwriting, and the two, shredded halves sitting on a pile of wet lettuce and grated carrots at the bottom of the garbage can. My name is ripped exactly in two. *Fi. Fi.* Gross that Aunt Gayle read it in that condition.

Letters were always Joanne-the-mother's game with me, when she was drunk or high or even just stressed out over the bills. Teary, non-sensical, overly analytical, weirdly short or bizarrely rambling. Or once, memorably blank, just my name at the top and a long scrawl where the pen drew down the page as her hand slid off the table. She must have passed out before she got any further on that one.

I learned not to read them.

And I know suddenly that I don't want to read anything from her right now. I don't want to see her. I don't want to hear from her. I don't want to talk to her. I realize with surprise that there's a rage boiling around the center of my chest.

A group therapist at Jennie's said there are two kinds of anger: the anger that holds you back, and the anger that spurs you on.

Which is mine?

The rest of the day is very quiet, and Aunt Gayle and Sadie keep an eye on me, while not wanting to seem to be watching me. I wander through the racks for a while, and I see Sadie pop past me, at the end of the row. Or I sit quietly at the desk in the bedroom that is mine, looking out the window, and Aunt Gayle drops by with a cup of tea.

It's okay, you two. I'm still here. Juggers is the only one who doesn't seem worried. He sits in a slice of sunshine on the bed near me, but not touching. Never touching.

I'm still a little dazed, I guess you can't lose twelve hours of your life without a weird, disorienting effect on you. I feel like I've overslept, or maybe had a lot of work done at the dentist and I'm still a little foggy. Not that I've had a lot of dental work done in my life, but I hear it can be hard on you.

This is exhausting. Leaving, coming back, being outside the rest of the world, trying to be part of it again.

After a while, though, I start to notice the noise from the shop below me.

It's the day before Halloween, and the store is popping.

So, very slowly, deliberately, I decide to rejoin humanity.

I slip into a clean pair of jeans and a white T-shirt, and I wander down to the main floor of the shop. Sadie is struggling under a pile of returns, and I appear beside her.

"Need help?"

"Yeah, these have all just been cleaned." She grins and splits her pile in two.

I stagger under a dozen heavy police uniforms and rehang them, by size and style. I take such care with each uniform, reveling in the stitches, the careful collars, the heavy, ornate buttons. There's a wool brush, and I brush each uniform carefully before placing the cardboard shoulder pads over them. Sadie says the pads are to keep them from fading.

Then I rehang party dresses: 1940s, 1950s, cocktail dresses, by size and decade. Beautiful colors, patterns, and material. It's almost too much, all this beauty.

Then I hang some of the novelty Halloween costumes. Monsters, Draculas, movie characters, which is fun and grounding. Still no lobsters.

It's mindless work, but physical. It's immensely calming and stress-free, plus there's something very satisfying about bringing order to all the messiness of clothes everywhere.

Moss Cart might really like this part of the job. The reorganizing, the structure, the rehanging.

I help Sadie do the returns for a few hours until my arms ache.

Then I help Edward replace burned out lightbulbs in the shop ceiling, which mostly is me standing at the bottom of the ladder, holding a box of lightbulbs. I go to see if Sylvia can use my help, although I know nothing about sewing machines so I don't see how, but when she sees me coming, she waves, smiles, and politely closes the sewing room door.

Brrrrr. Brrrrrr. Brrrrr.

Sheesh! What could be so secret in there? She has a mouthful of pins, so maybe she doesn't want to take them all out to talk to me?

People come into The Corseted Lady in little waves. Lunchtime and after school are busy. I see the little lamb and her Little Bo Peep mother near the end of the day.

"How'd it go?" I ask, as her mother hands me the costumes.

"Wonderful! We were the cutest mother and daughter at the party!" her mother beams.

The little girl rolls her eyes and whispers, "Mortifying." Her mother calls her to leave, and I give the girl props.

"Medieval warrior, next year," I say. She nods. "What are you going to be tomorrow?" she asks, and I look over at the novelty racks.

Still no lobsters.

"I'm not sure."

"See you next year then, I guess," she says, then drifts out the door behind her mother.

The end of the day comes, and it's been busy. Being busy has been good for me, I'm feeling a little more normal, a little more connected. It's been good for Aunt Gayle and Sadie too, I think. They are watching over me, but from a distance, with less hovering.

Which I like.

Aunt Gayle and I eat dinner, we watch more *Downton Abbey* on Netflix (and I have to agree with Aunt Gayle: the costumes are beautiful), we go to bed. It's all pretty normal, and I'm starting to feel a little more balanced.

No dissociation. No fugue state. No fugue music. No darkness at all.

We don't really talk too much, there's no need. And we don't talk about Joanne-the-mother, either.

Which is good. Which is fine by me. I can see there will be plenty of time to talk about her with Aunt Gayle. In fact, once I start therapy on Thursday, I'm sure she'll be all I talk about for a long time to come. Until I'm sick of talking about her.

But until then, we just don't.

And I get a good night's sleep, which is weird since I basically spent twelve hours the day before lying on the couch, but that wasn't really sleeping now was it?

It was lying in that black place I'd like to forget and try not to visit again.

No, I just sleep in my comfy nest on the floor. Juggers is on the bed. I roll over in my sleep once when I hear Aunt Gayle come in and look in on me, but that's it. Not even any dreams.

I sleep, then wake up slowly when Aunt Gayle taps on the door the next morning. She comes into the room for a second, something rattles gently, then she quickly walks out again.

"It's 7:30 — time for school, if you're up to it," she says. Then adds, "Happy Halloween!" from the hallway.

Something is flickering. Sunlight?

I slowly open my eyes. I blink. I blink again. I sit up. I rub my eyes.

A costume is hanging on a Rolling Judy at the end of the bed. I focus on it, blinking, trying to wake up.

Soft yellow lights gently flicker at me: on, off, on, off.

There's a Halloween costume hanging on the Rolling Judy.

And I think … no, wait, could it be?

IT IS!

I sit up and stare.

There on the Rolling Judy at the end of the bed, gently flashing in all its glory, is the most beautiful thing I've ever seen.

It's *a firefly costume!*

NINETEEN

Lit

I stand in front of the firefly costume for a long time, stilled, before I reach out to touch it.

The lights gently flicker inside the yellow mesh belly. There's a switch inside the right sleeve to turn them on and off. I stand in front of the Rolling Judy with this perfect firefly flickering at me for a long while.

I can barely breathe.

Then … I run my hand across the costume.

Hello.

The body is made out of brown and gold-red material, the lights flicker gently inside the yellow belly. The thorax goes down to what will probably be my knees. It's got six insect legs sticking out at the sides, and an insect head mask with a big bug jaw and antennae, but there's nothing over the eyes so I'll be able to see fine. Loose cloth wings hang down the back. There are shimmery, green-gold leggings and long, green leather lace-up boots to wear with it.

There's a handwritten note pinned to the long, red, undershirt sleeve. I unpin it.

For Firefly, So you can shine bright. Love AG + crew

I put the costume on slowly. Carefully. Mindfully.

The leggings, the red, long-sleeved undershirt, then the six-legged, winged suit, the head, then the boots. It's a lesson well-learned; next time, the boots go on before the suit. It's almost impossible to bend over to tie the bootlaces. I have to finally raise my leg to the bed and bend sideways to tie them.

But I do it, and when I'm fully suited, I look over at the mirror; I gasp.

I'm a Firefly.

Hard to dry tears in a firefly mask, so I try really hard not to cry.

But I wipe a few tears off my cheeks.

This beautiful costume. My aunt and her crew made it for *me*.

Now it makes sense why Sylvia was always shutting the door of the sewing room; I definitely recognize the material she was working on over the past few days.

Edward had small, flickering lights like the ones in the firefly belly in his hands last Saturday. I recognize Sadie's handiwork in the legs and antennae, and I realize that the idea must have occurred to her when we were hiding from Sharlene Baker in the Volkswagen Microbus. The day I said I could be a lobster for Halloween.

I get a little verklempt, and look at myself in the mirror for a long time.

I am an *awesome* firefly. I flicker the lights in my belly on and off.

It's perfect. And someone — everyone — cared enough to make it for me.

I sniffle enough that Juggers looks annoyed and takes off out the bedroom door without a backward glance. So, I stop sniffling.

I could not love this costume any more than I do at this moment.

There were fireflies all along the bushes in the park. Whenever I slept out there with Moss Cart nearby, when the house was too wild with screaming or crying or Joanne-the-mother breaking things, the fireflies were always there, flickering. I could watch them from the park bench, whenever I wanted, no matter what else was going on in the house, at sunset the fireflies filled the air, sparking and glowing. They were mine, beautiful, safe in the dark, all summer long.

I take one last look at myself, take a deep breath, then waddle out of the apartment.

I have to take the stairs slowly; this costume is NOT built for stairs. The thorax at my knees keeps me from bending too deeply. But I stop a few stairs down, because

I see Sadie, Sylvia, Edward, and Aunt Gayle waiting expectantly at the bottom.

They all see me and start clapping and smiling.

They gaze up at me, standing above them in the beautiful suit they made for me. They look genuinely happy to see me in their gift.

It's like a moment in *Downton Abbey* when someone floats down the castle stairs in something spectacularly gorgeous, and everyone at the bottom holds their breath in amazement before bursting into applause.

For a moment, as I look down at them all, I catch a glimpse of what they see: a strange, beautiful, half-hidden creature, lit from the inside.

It's almost too much for me.

I'm a lucky, lucky bug.

TWENTY

Halloween Yaraea

I get to the bottom of the stairs and Sadie high-fives me.

Aunt Gayle fusses that the costume fits me properly, and expertly checks the tight spots at my armpits and butt. Sylvia smiles and says, "You almost saw it yesterday!" and I laugh. I nod.

"Yeah, I wondered why you were always shutting the sewing room door!"

"The lights work okay?" Edward asks, and I nod and show him I've figured out how to turn them on and off with the switch in the sleeve.

For a moment we are all there together, happy, checking the firefly costume.

Then Aunt Gayle says it's time for breakfast, and do I want to go to school? And I do.

I do want to go to school.

So I eat some Cheerios in my costume, and everyone goes back to work. Sadie takes a few pictures of me in the firefly costume and posts them on The Corseted Lady Instagram account — with my permission, of course.

Aunt Gayle sits at the kitchen table, sewing a patch on a jacket sleeve.

"Aunt Gayle?" Munch, munch, mmmm Cheerios.

"Yep?" She looks up.

"I love the costume."

She nods, smiles.

"I love it, too." She takes a drag of her cigarette, blows it out, smiles again, laughs a little, goes back to sewing.

We're both a little embarrassed. It's hard not to be emotional. There's so much emotion waiting nearby that I think neither of us is too ready to jump into it. Not yet.

Next week, maybe.

There's a bulging lunch bag for me, and Aunt Gayle says, "Come home for lunch if you want, but you and Charlie might want to hang out or something. Up to you. It's Halloween. Have fun!"

I say thanks, then head outside. It's Halloween day, and it's a gorgeous, sunny morning, just a touch of crisp autumn in the air.

I walk along Queen Street in my firefly costume. I hit the switch in my sleeve and flicker the lights at people.

Little kid crying. Flick the firefly lights. Kid starts to smile.

Guy in a suit and a briefcase. Flick the firefly lights. Get a serious businessman to smile.

Streetcar driver. Flick the lights as I cross the street in front of the streetcar. He smiles and waves.

Guy in front of the Shoppers Drug Mart, with the Tim Hortons cup. Drop a few of Aunt Gayle's coins in the cup, flick the lights. Guy smiles and tells me to have a nice day.

I have to get used to walking in the firefly costume, but it's *definitely hilarious!*

This costume. This costume. I will never forget this day.

I get to school and pretty much everyone has a costume on. Some people are muted: there are some kitten ears and rabbit noses. There are some goth kids, and I see plenty of monsters and vampires, even a couple of clowns, which makes me shy away.

And a carrot.

Charlie is a really cute carrot, I must say. I get to my locker after Math, and he's waiting there in the carrot costume. He's kind of blocking my locker, though, so I say hello and push him out of the way.

There's another message on my locker: YOUR NAME IS FIFI.

I puzzle at this. How would anyone know what my name is?

"You should take a picture and tell someone this

time," Charlie says. He takes his cellphone out and takes a picture.

"I don't have a cellphone, remember? And there's nothing really threatening in telling me my name." Then I wipe the stupid comment off my locker. Who wrote it? *Firefly Freak* didn't bother me last time, but this does, even though I pretend it doesn't.

This time, it seems more personal.

Who knows about Fifi?

I erase it, it is black chalk, which I now have on my hands. I clap them together, and Charlie hands me a tissue. I wipe them off.

"Nice costume," he grins. "Firefly?"

I flicker the lights at him, and his eyes get big.

"It's *gorgeous*," he whispers. "Wow, your aunt is really talented."

"You like? Actually, I think it was a group effort. Sadie did the antennae and the legs. And probably the mask, too. Sylvia sewed the body. Edward did the lighting. Aunt Gayle was the mastermind."

I do a little twirl — well, a slow, waddly turn more than a real twirl — lights a-flicker.

Charlie and I go to French class. Leah looks pretty great as a member of a seventies, Australian heavy metal band. "AC/DC," she says, and I laugh.

So, a musical band, not electricity!

And Charlotte is wearing a huge, fluffy white cat costume that zips up the back. Frankly, it's freaking me out. Her green eyes are huge, inside an even bigger head. She's into cosplay, apparently, and I think that's one more reason to give her a wide berth. But that's not fair of me. What have I been doing lately if not costume play?

We're supposed to talk about Halloween in French. Charlie and I talk about our costumes … and what is the word for firefly? Insecte lumière? Le feu insecte? I have no idea, until Madame Frances comes to help: "Luciole. Or, in Canada, we also say, mouche à feu," she tells us.

Then Charlie and I have lunch together. Aunt Gayle is right, it is a gorgeous day, so we sit in the park at the edge of the back field and eat and chat.

Just a friendly firefly and a cute carrot having lunch.

After lunch, we go to our separate classes. I flash my firefly lights at people every once in a while, and every time I get a smile. Every time.

I make sure the nice lady in the principal's office gets a light flash, and she laughs so hard, I check to make sure she's okay. Then she takes my picture and asks if she can post it on the school's Twitter account. I tell her sure, but to tag The Corseted Lady so they can see their creation at school.

Sadie will love that!

I get to sit in the library for my last period. Charlie is there in his carrot costume.

Miss Turner has us all sit in a circle. I ask to sit on a chair because I honestly can't imagine sitting on the floor in this costume — I'll never get down there and I'll never get back up — so we all sit on chairs. Charlie sits beside me.

I realize that Miss Turner, Charlie, and I are the only ones in costume.

It also slowly dawns on me that not all of the other kids sitting in the library circle are familiar with Halloween. No one else is dressed up but us three. And why are we sitting in a circle anyway?

What's there to talk about?

I start to get a little uneasy. Something about this seems very … familiar.

It's only my second time sitting with these kids, and I haven't really looked at them before. The last time I was here in the library with them I had just remembered reading *OWL* magazine with Joanne-the-mother, so I wasn't really noticing much else.

Other than Charlie and me, I guess this group is mostly new Canadian kids, or kids who don't celebrate Halloween.

We all sit in our chairs.

"Firefly, did your aunt make you that fabulous costume?" Miss Turner asks.

"She sure did," I say, and flash the lights a few times.

Flicker, flicker.

"So, you and Charlie know about Halloween, but everyone else here is new to Halloween. Do you mind explaining Halloween a little?" Miss Turner is wearing a floppy hat, a flannel shirt under overalls, with straw under the hat and at her arms. Scarecrow.

"Sure, okay, Halloween," I start. "Um, even though it may seem scary, it's lighthearted. It starts when you're little. You dress up as a witch, or a bumblebee or a ghost, and wander around the neighborhood with your parents and friends. You go door to door and ask for candy."

Unless you're me, I think. *After I was six, I almost never went out for Halloween. I turned the lights out and pretended no one was home. What was happening inside the house was way scarier than anything happening outside.*

One boy sitting near me raises his hand.

"Yes, Omar?" Miss Turner asks.

"Candy? Like *sweet* candy?" Omar's English is clear, but it's not his first language. And as I look at him, I realize his other hand, the one in his lap … is a fake.

His right hand is *fake*? I look away from his hand, rattled a little, gather my composure.

"Uh, yeah, that's right. Chocolate bars, candy, bags of chips, gum. That kind of thing."

The girl Miss Turner was tutoring last time I was here puts her hand up.

"Yes, Faizah?" Faizah looks at me.

"Do you have fun doing this?" Her English is faltering,

but she gets it out. Does she think I'm foolish, dressing up in this way? It must seem kind of stupid. I have a creeping suspicion suddenly.

There's a box of tissues resting on an empty chair beside Miss Turner.

I realize I have sat in group therapy sessions at Jennie's, in a circle just like this, with other teenagers. And what are the tissues for if not for tears? I mean, it's too early in the year for cold and flu season.

It hits me.

We're a *support* group! This library class is literally *called* Library Support Group!

I take a better look around me. Charlie looks at me, raises his eyebrows in his carrot face.

There are Omar and Faizah, plus three more kids, two girls and a boy, and they all look lost. That's the best way I can describe it. One girl has a set of crutches beside her.

I feel really wobbly all of a sudden. My chest tightens, I have to remind myself to breathe.

Miss Turner senses my confusion.

"Everyone in this library support group is a survivor of a traumatic event, Firefly. When Mrs. Hazelle asked, I thought you'd fit with us. For now, anyway. There wasn't any room anywhere else."

Library *support* group. I thought it was support for homework. I swallow.

Survivors. Sure. Trauma survivors. Kids with PTSD and bad dreams.

Like me.

But why's Charlie here?

My chest tightens. I still have both hands. No crutches. I've slept in the park because it was safer than my house, watched my mother swing a baseball bat at cops, been caught by a social worker lately maybe, but what have these kids been through?

I look over at Charlie again, who looks solemn. Me. These kids. Now Charlie. What has he suffered?

I look at Faizah. I nod.

"Yes, Faizah, I do have fun doing this. It's fun to dress up as something else. Or someone else." I feel … tears. Oh no, please don't cry! I swallow hard.

Miss Turner comes to my rescue. She's good, her timing is perfect. "I'm a scarecrow. Charlie is a carrot. Does anyone want to guess what Firefly is dressed as?" Miss Turner says nicely, and I flash my lights.

Omar puts up his hand again, and says, "She is a flashing bug. One of those bugs in the grass when the sun sets and the evening comes. I have seen them, we had them where I used to live."

Miss Turner smiles. "Is that right, Firefly? Are you a flashing bug in the grass?"

I nod. I flash my lights, but I'm overcome. I just can't speak, and kind Miss Turner forges on ahead for me.

"Yes! Firefly is a firefly! That's what we call them in Canada."

Omar grins.

He has a faraway look in his eyes.

"Yaraea. That is what we called them." The other kids in the circle nod, and I swear they all smile.

Then I flash my lights, and for a moment the room is filled with giggling trauma survivors.

Okay. Fireflies light up the room anywhere, I guess.

And I'm not the only survivor who has seen them flashing in the darkness, and thought they were beautiful.

TWENTY-ONE

Bridges

L ibrary survivor group (forget the "support," I'm calling it what it is) is over and after learning about yaraea, I honestly feel just a touch better. I manage to regain some composure as I saunter with Charlie to my locker. Last class of the day is music.

I'm not going to make it to music. At least, not this week.

Charlie has a spare, and it seems I just can't say no to him.

Such an adorable carrot.

So instead of music, I make a break for it. We walk out of Leslie Street Central High School, a firefly and a carrot. We're not the only ones leaving early. It's Halloween. A steady stream of kids in costumes sneak off across the parking lot, across the street, like us.

Charlie and I walk along Queen Street. I get right to the point.

"What were you doing in that library group? I mean, I guess you know I've had a tough few months, but what about you?"

"It's a long story," Charlie says. I nod politely. He doesn't offer any more and I don't press. If those support groups at Jennie's taught me anything, "it's a long story" is code for "I just can't, not right now."

"Do you want to go trick-or-treating?" he asks.

"I don't care what you think, we are definitely too old to go out trick-or-treating. Besides, I haven't gone trick-or-treating in a long time," I say.

We walk quietly a while longer, then I blurt out, "How did Omar lose his hand?"

"I'm not sure. He hasn't talked about it." Then he says, "Well, we could walk around and watch little kids going trick-or-treating, then. Just for fun."

This conversation is hard to keep together, it's too far to either end of existence. A boy losing a hand somehow.

Deciding whether or not to go trick-or-treating.

I blink, trying to hold it together, then shake my head.

"No. We can't watch kids go trick-or-treating. Too lurk-y. How about this. You know where I live, but I know absolutely nothing about you. How about we go to your place for Halloween night and hand out candy? Introduce me to the family ... the group of other humans that you probably live with?"

A group of kids dressed as four Hobbits walk past. They have elven cloaks, curly wigs and slightly pointed ears, little blue, plastic swords, and each kid is looking at their cellphone.

I flicker my lights at them, and they don't even notice.

"Off to Isengard?" I ask, but no one looks up. "Tough crowd," I mutter. Moss Cart had a copy of *The Lord of the Rings* in his shopping cart, and I read it obsessively all summer long.

Then Charlie says, "You don't want to go to my house, Firefly."

"Why?"

His face in the carrot mask is still.

The Unknowable Carrot.

Great title for a video series, I think. But I can tell he's serious, and sad about something.

"The same reason you were at the library group for trauma survivors?" I flash my lights at him. I'm being callous, jaunty, with this information. Charlie ignores me.

"It isn't that much fun at my house. Believe me, no one is handing out candy." He hesitates and takes a long look at me. I grow solemn; that face is sweet but sad.

"There's a place I do want you to see, though. Can you walk in that?" he asks.

The firefly costume is actually okay for walking — I've gotten used to it. It's just not so great on stairs. I nod.

"Let's go then."

So we walk along Queen, past all the little kids leaving school in their adorable bumblebee and pumpkin Halloween costumes. A few people honk at us as they drive past, and I flicker my lights. Some people honk again.

We grab two large mint teas (I've decided to cut down on coffee), and I get a slice of poppyseed cake, and we walk slowly up Broadview to Danforth. It's such a glorious day, not too hot, not too cold, and the city shines off to the west. The trees in the Don Valley are in full autumn colors.

People walk past us, dressed in various costumes. Superheroes are really in this year. I don't see any lobsters, though. Everyone smiles at the firefly and the carrot. I give the firefly lights a flicker again and again, and people smile even more. I get a few high-fives and thumbs-up from complete strangers on the sidewalk.

I tell a few people I got the costume at The Corseted Lady, when they ask.

"Where are we going?" I ask a few times, but Charlie just says, "You'll see."

So I stop asking.

After a while, we arrive at the Bloor Street Viaduct. They call it Viaduct, but really it's just a huge bridge over the Don Valley. Charlie walks ahead of me, and a bunch of jerks in a taxi call out the window, "CARROT TOP IS STUPID!!" but he doesn't pay attention to them.

He walks halfway along the concrete wall of the bridge and stops. He leans against the wall, looks down into the valley below us.

Traffic is building, since it's almost rush hour.

Cars zoom past us on the bridge, and on the highway below us, way down there on the Don Valley Parkway, driving fast, north out of the city, south into it. The sun is low in the sky to the west, the CN Tower blinks at us. They've programmed spiders to climb the tower tonight, and from this distance, they really are creepy.

I catch up with Charlie, lean against the wall, and we look down together on the cars speeding north and south.

"What are we doing here?" I ask again. I flash my lights at a bus zooming past on Danforth, and all the people inside look at me. Some smile. A little kid dressed as Spiderman grins and waves. A few other people walk past on the bridge, but it's mostly just cars and buses zooming by.

Charlie looks at me, and his carrot-face is scrunched up. Sad.

"Firefly … I know you were saying something important in French class as Boy Two the other day. For that stupid coffee shop dialogue. Plus, you're in Miss Turner's library group for trauma survivors. And I know it's something about your mother. You … well … did you live on the street or something? Is that true?" He blurts the last part out, like he can't hold it in any longer.

I let a few beats pass. I flash my firefly lights at him.

I sigh.

"Yeah. Well, I didn't live on the street really. But sometimes I *slept* in a park across the street from my house. Technically, I lived with my mother."

"Did you run away or something?"

Kinda nosy there, Charlie, I think. But then … I hear a therapist at Jennie's saying, "Telling people isn't weak, Firefly. It's the truth. Just tell the *right* people. The ones who will actually hear you."

I lean over the bridge wall, stare down at the dizzying wall of speeding cars below. Then turn my back to the traffic and lean my elbows on the wall. I nod.

"I didn't run away, the park was right across the street from her house. I hid there when I needed to. When it was safer than sleeping at home. I had a friend there who watched over me. Moss Cart. He lived on the street. Sweet guy, a little messed up."

There's a long pause. Charlie wants to say something to me, but I don't think he can get the words out. Tears fill his eyes.

That's the problem with telling the truth.

This is one of the reasons I don't tell anyone much about myself: it makes them cry. At least one therapist at Jennie's cried the first time I showed up last year. They always stopped crying, though, when I told them I wasn't coming back if anyone cried again.

Charlie starts to speak: "Well, I ... I ... I ..." he revs. He's rocking a little, stuck.

I put my firefly hand on his carrot arm. "Charlie, it's okay. Is there a reason we're standing on this bridge? Does it have anything to do with a traumatic incident?" I try to sound lighthearted, like Miss Turner.

He nods hard, and his carrot foliage rattles around his face.

My heart starts to thud, just a little harder.

"What happened, Charlie?" But he can't speak, he just shakes.

The traffic on the Don Valley Parkway below us is loud. Car horns, tires, revving of traffic at high speed. It's not all that nice actually. I'd like to get out of here. Suddenly, I wonder what Aunt Gayle and Sadie are doing back at the shop.

Charlie swallows hard.

"Maybe we should go," I say. I'm actually getting really nervous standing here. What's wrong with Charlie? "I'm hungry, anyway. Let's go get something to eat." I try to be as calming as I can.

Charlie is full on crying now, silent tears stream down his cheeks.

"Charlie, it's okay."

He coughs, then looks at me. He shakes his head and his foliage rattles. Tears, and snot now, too. "She ... she got hit. On her bike. Right here." His voice is strangled, a whisper.

I stare at him for a minute, not getting it.

"Who got hit on her bike?" I say.

Charlie looks at me, then whispers, "My mom. Right here."

I'm bewildered, but slowly I get it. Charlie's mom got hit on her bike. Right here.

Did she ... where is she now? I can't ask, but Charlie's body language says everything.

"Your mom? On her bike?" It's all I can say, disbelieving.

I blink a few times, and Charlie nods, then his carrot face really crunches up and he starts to cry. Hard. I put my hand on his shoulder, then he swings into me for a hug.

Oh no. NONONO! Charlie's mother *died* on this bridge?

He cries into me. It's not all that easy to hug someone when you've got antennae and six bug legs out the side. But I do hold on to him, even though I'm not a hugger. Even when perfectly nice therapists at Jennie's offered me a hug, I never, ever wanted one. I let him sob.

My heart screws up a little and starts to beat in my throat. I try to take a few steadying breaths. I keep hugging him, letting him run tears and snot onto the top of my firefly costume.

Cars go past, honking at us. *Shut up!*

"Charlie … that's just … I'm so sorry." It's all I can think of to say.

A social worker came calling, my mother swung a baseball bat at a cop, and that ended in me getting snatched by Sharlene Baker.

But Charlie's mother died on this bridge.

Right here.

After a few more moments of clinging to me, he straightens up and wipes his nose on the orange gloves. He hiccups gently.

"A truck hit a patch of black ice. She died right away, fast, on this spot." He takes a deep breath, swallows, puts his hand on the concrete barrier in front of us.

"I was ten. I took months off school. I had a therapist for a long time. I think I need to go back. I'm having these terrible dreams …"

"I'm sorry … I really am," I say again. Then add, "I know what you mean about the dreams."

Charlie takes a breath, sighs, then hiccups a little. He looks so broken.

Then he seems kind of resigned, sighs once more. "I don't want to take you to my house for other reasons, though. My stepmother will be there. I really don't like her."

"Well, I can honestly say that I doubt I will ever have to deal with a stepparent. I just don't see it happening for Joanne-the-mother," I say. He looks at me.

"Not that many opportunities to meet Mr. Right in CAMH, I guess," he says, then kind of half grins.

When Carrots Smirk.

I smile a little. "Probably not, but with Joanne, you never know. Come on, let's go."

But Charlie shakes his head.

"No. We have to do something first. We get to say one thing to our mothers, standing right here. So the bridge gods can hear. Something we wished we'd said."

"My mom is still alive, Charlie, if currently incarcerated in a mental health institute," I protest, but he shakes his head. A bus whizzes by, and we can't hear each other for a second, but Charlie is solemn.

"No, we have to. I've done it before alone, lots of times. It helps. I'll go first." He thinks for a moment, starts slowly.

He locks eyes with me. Suddenly, I can't look away.

"Mom, when I was little, I always hoped it didn't hurt. I wanted it … not to hurt you. Getting hit by a truck. I used to dream about a big cloud swallowing you up before you felt any pain. A fluffy cloud coming out of the sky to cushion you."

Intense, Charlie. We both spend a little time with the thought of a big fluffy cloud coming to soften the pain for his mother. On this bridge. Right here. It's exactly what a ten-year-old boy would think, I realize. He wanted to protect his mother, the only way he could.

With something soft and fluffy. My heart feels like a hand is squeezing it, wringing out all the blood in it. I try to breathe, very slowly.

"Now you," he says.

What am I going to say? I nod. Breathe out. Swallow.

"Okay, well …" I think about it. There are too many things to say to Joanne-the-mother, and she's not dead. I can still say these things to her face if I ever speak to her again. Looking at Charlie who can't ever speak to his mother again, I start to think that maybe, one day, I will speak to Joanne.

I'll have to. I have things to say.

Charlie looks at me, his big eyes unblinking in his carrot face. Drying tears streak his cheeks.

Where to start? I look up at the bridge supports, way above my head. If Charlie can do it, I guess I can.

I start, shaky.

"Joanne. You were a crap Mom." Charlie nods encouragement at me, so I go on. "I didn't have a childhood because of you. I brought you water, I fed you, I covered you with blankets, and cleaned up after you since I was six. After Dad left. I lied to the neighbors, to the school, to everyone for you. But no more. From now on, I take care of myself, not you. And no more lying."

There. Really, I've just repeated what the therapists at Jennie's said to me over and over. Maybe it's finally sinking in.

Charlie looks at me in wonder, then whispers, "Anything else?"

I sigh. I wasn't expecting to have so much to say, but apparently, there's still more. All this honesty and talking feels sort of like throwing up: you feel terrible doing it, but so much better afterward.

"Joanne, the hardest part is sometimes, when you had a job and stability, you really tried. We weren't always poor. You weren't always drunk or stoned. You didn't always sell my stuff for rent or drug money. I just wish I had more good memories of us."

Charlie nods, satisfied. I guess I'm finally done with the word vomit. "Okay. Good. Now, we spit!"

"Spit?" I ask.

I'm pretty sure a sign somewhere behind me says: NO THROWING OBJECTS FROM BRIDGE. Does spit count? But Charlie nods, and I can't say no.

So we both lean out over the bridge, and on three, we hork as hard as we can out into the air. Honestly, it's not that easy in a firefly costume, but I hold the insect jaws open wide and let loose with a wad.

Two splats of hork land on a pick-up truck bed of tires heading north.

I owe Joanne-the-mother that much.

Then we head back down Broadview toward Queen Street.

I flash my lights at cars, and as the sun goes down, my

flickering lights really stand out. People honk, smile, wave, high-five me. They see me. Firefly.

A beacon of light in the dark.

TWENTY-TWO

Flicker

Charlie and I sit on stools in a Greek take-out place. I really love Greek food. Like, yum. Just stuff me with feta, black olives, and bread and I'll be happy for the rest of my life.

We haven't talked much about the bridge since we left it. It's behind us, for now. It'll be ahead of us, again, we both know that. We'll be talking to our mothers across one bridge or another for the rest of our lives, I guess.

But right now, we're eating Greek food.

It's actually really good to share a little with Charlie. It's been such a sad few months that I realize I haven't talked very much to anyone except Moss Cart, and the therapists at Jennie's. And over the past week, Aunt Gayle, Sadie, and Sharlene Baker.

I mean, I haven't talked to anyone my own age for a

while. In those group sessions at Jennie's, I listened but hardly spoke. I just don't like sharing. And most of those kids were a lot older than me. I was always worried that I'd slip up, say something about being in grade eight and prove I wasn't sixteen, and get kicked out. Or caught by a social worker.

Which happened anyway, I realize suddenly. The getting caught part, anyway. Someone finally contacted the local social workers about me although I'll probably never know who. The landlord? A neighbor? Someone from my class who did see me sleeping out in the park? Maybe Moss Cart knows. One more question for him if I ever see him again.

"What's your best class?" Charlie asks, around a mouthful of Greek potatoes. His chewing makes the carrot leaves around his face wobble, and it's actually hilarious.

When Carrots Eat.

"You mean in school?" I stab some rice and olives into my mouth. He nods.

"I don't know. I guess if I had to choose … I probably am best at math. What about you?"

"English, I'm a pretty good writer."

A skinny streak of skin whizzes by the restaurant window.

Another streak whizzes by, a bigger streak. No skin.

I jump up, and my firefly suit knocks over a plastic chair behind me. Everyone in the restaurant looks over at me, then back at their food. Charlie stops mid-chew, raises an eyebrow.

"What?"

"Come on!" I wrap up what's left of my food, toss it into the garbage, and run — well, waddle — out onto Queen Street. Charlie catches up to me.

"What is it?" he asks again, and I point down Queen Street.

"That kid, what did you call him? Scott someone, Dunkin? Drunkin? Durkin? He just ran past, with Norman whatever chasing him. Come on!"

"What are we going to do if we catch up with them?" he asks.

"I don't know! We'll think of something!"

Charlie is fast. He starts sprinting along Queen Street ahead of me, and I really can only waddle. It's a fast waddle, maybe, but there's just no running in a firefly costume. He's a block ahead of me in seconds.

Charlie, though, is the fastest carrot I've ever seen. Well, okay, he's the ONLY carrot I've ever seen at a sprint. He pelts along, and he's tall anyway, but with the carrot top and the foliage above his head, he looks like a weird, runaway giraffe. People on the sidewalk start to part the crowd for him, little kids point and smile.

When Carrots Sprint.

He stops two blocks ahead of me, and I come puffing up.

"I guess I lost them?" he says, not even out of breath. I bend over, put my hands on my knees, try to catch my breath. I am never smoking again, not ever.

"Are you on the track team or something?" I gasp. He nods.

"Well, I always see them in front of the Shoppers Drug Mart, I guess let's go look there."

So we trot and waddle along, and get to the Shoppers, but they're not there. It's fully dark out now, and Halloween is in full swing. Kids roam the street in squads, most of them in costumes. Everyone is jacked up on sugar, and I have to say the street has a weird vibe. Snatches of conversation sound like buzzing bees. Sometimes, from people in bee costumes. It's a little disorienting.

Then a sensible, blue, four-door sedan pulls around the corner and heads north on Carlaw.

"What time is it?" I demand, and Charlie pulls out his cellphone.

"It's uh, 8:35."

"Oh no! That social worker, I totally forgot she was coming tonight! Come on!"

I rush-waddle around the corner of the Shoppers Drug Mart, head past the coffee shop into the parking lot across from The Corseted Lady and stop.

I catch a glimmer of skin. Someone ducks behind the garbage cans lining the laneway behind the pharmacy. I take a few steps toward the garbage cans and call out.

"Scott? Scott Durkin? Is that you?"

Nothing. Charlie stands patiently with me, looking around.

"Scott! It's Firefly! Firefly Warren! And Charlie …" I look at Charlie. I have no idea what his last name is.

"From school!"

Nothing. No answer.

I take a few more steps toward the garbage cans. There is nothing but darkness there. I flash my lights, on off, on off, and a head peeks above the cans, then ducks back.

It IS Scott.

I'm about to call out to him again when …

… suddenly light spills partway into the parking lot from across the lane. The front door to The Corseted Lady opens, and Aunt Gayle stands there. She lets Sharlene Baker into the shop. The door closes and the parking lot is dark again.

"Scott!" I call out. "It's okay, come on out!"

I flash my lights some more. Flicker, flash, on off, on off.

A body swings around the side of the pharmacy.

Uh-oh.

Not-So-Skinny Kid runs around the side of the pharmacy and skids to a halt in the parking lot.

Norman whatever. Jacks? Jakes? He stops. He sees us.

One thing about flickering lights: they do attract attention. What have I done?

He sneers at us.

Heads toward us.

"Stop!" I say. For some reason, I flicker my firefly lights like crazy. It's my superpower.

I flicker the lights and it's one part hilarious, and one part possibly really stupid.

I've done a little reading about fireflies: I think they do flash when they're in danger. Mostly during mating season though. But possibly when they're in danger too. Anyway, it seems perfectly normal to flicker my lights. And it does seem to bedazzle Norman.

He stops. He stares at me.

"What? Are you … are you *seriously* dressed as a firefly?" He seems amazed. Almost bewildered. Too bewildered to attack.

Caught off guard, just enough to stall for time.

"Yeah. So what?" I keep flickering my lights, and he seems unsure what to do. It's my force field. I'm buying time. I have no idea why I can't stop flickering, or what's going to happen next.

Flicker. Flicker. Flicker.

"Hi *Fifi*," he says, mocking.

"That is my name, yes. And that's you writing on my locker, isn't it? Why don't you just stop picking on people? It's stupid."

Flicker. Flicker. Flicker.

Norman looks like he'd like to take a swipe at me, but

maybe it's just not possible to take a swipe at a flickering firefly. Maybe flickering lights really *are* a good defense mechanism? Charlie stands uneasily, tall and orange, between us.

"Stop it, Jakes, you're being an idiot. You're just going to get in a lot of trouble," he says, quietly.

Then Aunt Gayle opens the shop door again and peers out.

I see Sharlene Baker in the shadow behind her. Shop light streams out onto the sidewalk, spills into the parking lot, a halo of golden light. We're still in darkness, though, behind the pharmacy.

I take a step toward the shop, call out, "Aunt Gayle!" Flicker, flicker.

"Firefly?" she calls into the darkness, but she turns my way. She sees my lights in the dark.

And Scott Durkin sees his escape. He bolts from behind the garbage cans and tears toward the open shop door.

He's fast.

He's got no shoes, no shirt. Just baggy track pants. Norman Jakes takes a short run after him, reaches out, but Scott is faster.

"Scott! Norman!" Sharlene Baker shouts from the doorway, surprised. Norman Jakes stops, hears her, sees her. His eyes get huge, and fearful, and he turns and bolts back out to Queen Street.

Scott runs straight into the shop.

He's so fast, he just bolts right past Aunt Gayle and Sharlene Baker into The Corseted Lady before Aunt Gayle realizes what's happening. She turns, sees him, then looks back out into the darkness for me, puzzled. Charlie and I trot and waddle up.

"Hi, Aunt Gayle," I say, and she says hi, still puzzled. Her face has a definite *What is GOING ON?* look.

Scott Durkin is standing beside the counter, looking at us all, terrified, dazed. Shoeless. Shirtless.

Sharlene Baker manages another surprised, "Scott!"

We're all frozen for a moment, a weird tableau in drama class that would be difficult to caption: *shoeless, shirtless boy pelts past confused adults into costume shop while insect-girl and carrot-boy look on.*

Then without a word, Aunt Gayle walks over, reaches into a bag of clothes beside the counter, and hands Scott Durkin a clean plaid shirt.

It's the most beautiful thing I've ever seen.

TWENTY-THREE

When Carrots Read

Scott Durkin is about to leave the shop, fully clothed. He and Sharlene Baker are heading out to find Norman Jakes and to start a full stepfamily intervention and intensive family therapy.

And possibly to press charges.

I don't know for sure, though, but that's the gist of what I overhear.

Scott sits on one of the overstuffed couches, while Sharlene Baker makes some hurried phone calls on her cell in the privacy of Aunt Gayle's office. Sharlene Baker shouts things like, "Yes! He's here right now!" and "Calm down, please, Mrs. Durkin," loudly enough for us all to hear through the office doors.

Charlie and I stand beside Scott; a carrot and a firefly trying to be supportive.

"Hi Scott, I'm Firefly. This is Charlie," I say. I flicker my lights a few times. He notices, but doesn't seem to register what I'm doing. I recognize that dazed look. What I looked like when I first arrived here ten days ago, probably.

"Hi," he answers. Aunt Gayle comes over to the couches with a bag of clothes plus a pair of work boots and heavy gray socks. I think she knit them a few nights ago. He pulls the socks on, slowly, painfully does up the boots.

"There's a hoodie and some undershirts in there," she says, handing him the bag of clothes.

"Thanks," he says, doing everything in slow motion.

It hurts, I know, coming back to the world.

Sharlene Baker walks up, drops her cellphone into her purse. Then she takes out an envelope, hands it to Aunt Gayle. She tries to hide it, but I see who it's for.

It says "Fifi" on it.

In Joanne-the-mother's handwriting.

Aunt Gayle hides it behind her back. Sharlene Baker snaps into Social Worker mode.

"Sorry Firefly, Gayle, we have to go. I have to help Scott. He's going to his uncle's for the night. His step-mother is freaking out. We have to find Norman before he hurts himself or anyone else. Can we reschedule for next week? I know you're starting therapy tomorrow, Firefly, so we'll check how that's going then. I'll call. Bye.

Come on, Scott." She says all this really fast, then turns to Aunt Gayle and says thank you.

Then she and Scott Durkin vanish out the door.

Gone.

I have to admit, there's suddenly something very comforting about those shoulder-padded, eighties power suits on the right, no-nonsense, tough-as-nails person. Thank you for your service, Sharlene Baker.

Aunt Gayle shuts the door behind her, and we all stay very still for a few moments. A kind of weird calm descends over us. The three of us just stand and look at each other, until Charlie flops down into the couch.

I flicker my lights a few times.

Then Aunt Gayle pulls the letter out from behind her back and says, "Do you want me to tear up this letter, Firefly?" She holds the letter close to her, and I think about it.

She could tear it up. I certainly don't want any more dissociation or weird, possible fugue states happening.

I look at the letter in Aunt Gayle's hand for a moment.

There's the Joanne-the-mother handwriting. The messy, familiar, all-too-intense possibility of whatever is in the letter.

But I'm here. I'm not going to vanish out of the world. Not tonight with Charlie and Aunt Gayle here, and me in my superpower firefly suit. There's a therapist out there somewhere in the world with my name and a file on their computer for our first meeting tomorrow. And I don't even have to pretend to be sixteen.

I shake my head. "No, I'm fine. Leave it on the table for me to read. Thanks, Aunt Gayle."

She looks at me worried, but then she nods a little.

"Okay, if you're sure. Your call. I'm making tea and scones. They'll be ready in fifteen." She turns and vanishes into the kitchen.

That was brave of you, Aunt Gayle, I think. She's letting me make my own decisions here, even though the last letter from Joanne-the-mother sent me into the darkness for twelve hours. She trusts me to know who I am, what's okay, and what's not.

She and I are going to be just fine.

I stand beside the couch in front of Charlie.

I ever-so-slowly pick up the envelope with the letter from Joanne-the-mother.

First, I fan my face with it, like it's really hot in here.

Then I play hot potato with it from hand to hand.

Then I drop kick it lightly across the shop floor. It lands near the *California Beach Bum: 1950s* rack.

Charlie watches silently.

I go and pick it up again.

I pretend to light it on fire and watch it burn up in flames while I dance around it like a maniac.

I drop it and shoot bullets at it from my finger-tip gun.

I dig an invisible knife into it on the floor and skin and gut it.

I mime tearing it into little pieces and throwing them up into the air and standing in the confetti rain of shredded letter.

I mime eating it, and gagging on the pieces, then pulling out a long, endless chain of scarves.

I bash it around a little with a billy club from the prop cupboard. Then I spend a few minutes keeping it airborne with a badminton racket.

I pull on a pair of huge cop boots and stomp on it, doing a weird little dance, legs out, arms crossed, head flopping from side to side. Like a doll maybe. Or a puppet on a string.

A puppet in a firefly suit.

This all goes on for a while, in complete silence, while Charlie watches with solemn eyes.

Then I finally pick it up, and flop onto the couch beside the boy in the carrot suit. The letter has withstood my war on it pretty well. It's still in one piece, anyway.

"Read this with me, would you?"

Charlie does a double-take. "Are you sure? Maybe that's not such a good idea, Firefly. I mean you just spent the last ten minutes blowing it up in a dozen ways."

"Yeah, that was necessary. But I'm sure, it's okay. I can read it now."

"Okay. Should we ... read it out loud?" He seems really

doubtful, but I know he'll read it with me. We horked off a bridge together tonight. No one can make this about them, not even Joanne-the-mother.

"No. Let's just read it quietly together."

I tear open the envelope. I carefully unfold the letter which is eccentrically over-folded down to a tiny piece of paper, classic Joanne-the-mother. I hold it open in my hands.

"Ready?" I ask. He nods.

"Read."

Dear Fifi,

The social worker says you are doing okay with Gayle. She'll take care of you. I'm glad to know you're safe. You probably won't believe this, but I actually feel good here. This is the longest I've gone without some drug — or alcohol or whatever else — in my system since I was about your age. The doctors tell me soon the meds will work and I'll feel more normal. I just have to try to remember what normal is.

There's some good news. They dropped the charges from the baseball bat night. I have to do some community service probably, but I'll be happy to.

But I don't expect you to forgive me, or be there for me. I know I let you down, in so many ways. I'll be here waiting for you, though, if you ever want to come to talk. I'll have more to say then. But I understand why you might not want to.

You deserved better, Fifi. I'm sorry and I love you.
Joanne

There is silence for a full thirty seconds after we both finish the letter.

Then Charlie clears his throat and says, "That's not what I expected."

"Yeah," I say. "She's scariest when she's rational."

But … a tiny voice in me says, I wonder.

I wonder if she'll actually find a way out of her addiction this time. I've wondered so long that I can't take any more time in my life wondering about her. I have to start thinking about me.

She's in a good place, though, for the first time since I've been old enough to think about it. I know there were even good times, now and then. The cover of *OWL* magazine pops into my head.

I guess we'll see. I'm not holding my breath, I'm not waiting for a miracle, but we'll see.

Then Charlie asks, "And *Fifi*? She didn't call you Firefly?"

I shake my head. "No, she didn't. I never told her my name was Firefly. It was mine alone, not hers. I don't expect you to understand that …"

He interrupts me. "No, I get it. You renamed yourself. Like a rebirth."

I smile at him. He does get it.

I fold the letter back up into its tiny, eccentric Joanne-fold, then stick it back into the envelope. I drop it on the table. Maybe Aunt Gayle wants to read it.

Then Aunt Gayle, Charlie, and I sit in the kitchen and eat blueberry scones and drink tea. Sadie and Max come in around 9:30 and join us. We sit around playing a game of Monopoly, all five of us, until it's late and Charlie has to leave.

Monopoly. There's something I haven't played in a long time. In fact, I don't think I've ever actually played Monopoly before. We had a Monopoly game once when I was little I think, but it was in pieces all over the place.

Sadie won, I came second, Charlie was out first.

After Monopoly, he gets out of his carrot costume and hangs it up on the returns rack.

I show him to the door, say goodnight, and a hand-shake isn't going to do it, so I go in for a quick hug. That's two hugs in one night.

For someone who doesn't really like hugging, I'm doing a lot of it.

I say goodnight after the hug, shut the door, head up

to the apartment. I say goodnight to Aunt Gayle, then disappear into the bedroom.

Slowly, I remove the Firefly costume.

I put it back on the Rolling Judy, which is still in the room. Unroll the green tights and feed them through the costume legs, tuck them into the green leather boots at the bottom. I hang the firefly mask on the Rolling Judy's wire head.

I turn on the firefly lights.

I sit on the edge of the bed in the darkness, and watch the flickering lights. They really are mesmerizing. It's a beautiful costume. I hope I can keep it in my room all the time. The thought of anyone else renting it or wearing it makes me a little mad.

I hope it's mine forever.

I can't imagine Aunt Gayle renting it out, though.

The door opens a little, and Juggers jumps up onto the bed. He looks at me, a little alarmed, but decides against jumping down. He walks to the very edge of the bed, closes his eyes, then stretches out beside me.

"Hi, stray cat," I mumble. There's no denying it. That cat IS purring.

It's been such a long day.

My mind drifts. A boy with a fake hand. A boy in a carrot suit leaning against a bridge, spitting into the void. A boy with no shirt.

My eyes open wide. Oh yeah! Somehow Norman Jakes

must have figured my name out through Sharlene Baker. She's competent, tough, but seriously overworked. An unlocked, bulging briefcase, an open file, even mentioning my real name in an overworked moment ... all possible.

I also realize that I don't care that much if Norman Jakes knows my other name is Fifi.

I yawn and lie down on the bed. I watch the firefly glow and listen to the rumble of a Juggernaut, purring at my feet.

Stray cat, stray cat, where your kitty-katty home be at?

In my sleepy state on the comfy bed, I hear Moss Cart singing his song. There was more to it though, I can almost hear it. What was it? I let my mind wander, and then it comes back to me.

Stray cat, stray cat, where your kitty-katty home be at?
Kitty wander, kitty roam, kitty-katty, here be home.

Then ... Juggers and I sleep on the bed until morning.

TWENTY-FOUR

Mostly Moss Cart

It's 11:45 p.m. on December 6th.

The final minutes of my birthday.

I'm in bed in the dark, watching the flickering firefly. Aunt Gayle is in the living room, sewing something. Juggers hasn't joined me yet; he's in the warehouse prowling for mice.

Long day.

This is the first birthday party I can actually remember. There were presents: a cellphone from Aunt Gayle, books from Sadie, a journal from Charlie. Aunt Gayle, Charlie, Sadie, Max, and I went to a movie, which was the second movie I've ever seen in my life.

It was a Star Wars story, which everyone seemed to love. I've never seen any of these movies so I didn't know the characters or what was going on, but it didn't matter. It was fun to be with everyone.

We came back to The Corseted Lady for dinner, Greek take-out food, and played Monopoly. Charlie stayed. Sharlene Baker dropped by. Edward, Sylvia, Sadie, Max, and a few more people were here for cake.

And Aunt Gayle. Always Aunt Gayle. I still don't like being the center of attention very much, but I'm not going to say no to a birthday party, am I?

So, what is fourteen going to be like? Frankly, thirteen didn't start out so well, but got quite a bit better.

For one thing, there's Charlie.

We've spent basically every day together since Halloween. It took a while, but I finally met his dad and stepmom, and he's right, she's not at all fun to be around.

Then there's therapy. I go once a week, which is fine. Hard. Necessary. Fine. The therapist is a perfectly nice person who seems to know exactly what to ask me to make me fall to pieces. Luckily, she's also pretty good at mopping up the mess. She signed me up for a street kids' group therapy session starting soon. Technically I wasn't exactly a street kid, I argue, the therapist got me onto the list anyway. A park bench, even part time, is the street, she says.

School is fine, I'm caught up now in everything. I've even been to Music Class, where I play the trombone. I'm terrible at it, just as terrible as everyone else anyway, and I don't even care what it sounds like. It's slightly hilarious.

I met my cousin Amanda, who came home for a weekend visit. She was amazing and fun. I was a little worried she was going to be mad at me, living in her apartment with her mother, wearing her old clothes, but she was only happy to see me. She's studying Women's Rights and International Law, I guess that's her specialty. Suddenly I'm wondering what law school might be like one day.

I help Aunt Gayle in The Corseted Lady every Sunday.

I'm starting to learn the inventory pretty well, even if there are seven million pieces.

After Halloween, we started a clothing drive at the shop. I've sorted through enough clothes bins at Jennie's to see how great the need is on the street, but after seeing how useful a handy plaid shirt can be for a shirtless kid, the idea popped into my head.

Each Sunday afternoon, Aunt Gayle and I sort through one small section of The Corseted Lady for a few hours and take out a few bags of clothes that someone might need. Then one Sunday a month we drop them off at Jennie's, where they are happy to get them and really happy to see me. Sometimes Charlie helps too.

The Corseted Lady has inventory that rarely gets rented out of the shop, especially seventies, eighties, and nineties stuff, T-shirts and plaid shirts and hoodies, and it's been fun watching Aunt Gayle discover pieces she'd completely forgotten about. She tells me where they came from and when. ("I bought this Davie Bowie T-shirt right after the Ziggy Stardust tour!") She decides if they are worth keeping: are they rentable anymore or not? If not and it's still something someone would actually wear, they go into the clothing drive bag. I also see her slip in a few items that she knit: hats, mittens, scarves, socks.

So, I'm doing okay.

No more dissociation or possible fugue states anyway, I'm happy to say.

But there are a few not-so-okay things.

A few Sundays ago, Aunt Gayle and I went grocery shopping. We had a bag of clothes to drop off at Jennie's. Between grocery shopping and dropping off the clothes …

… I saw a guy pushing a shopping cart along the side of the road, near Lakeshore.

"Stop the car!" I shouted. Aunt Gayle slammed on the brakes.

"What? What is it?" she asked, but I didn't answer. I jumped out and ran over to the guy … and it was him!

It was Moss Cart!

There were no *My Little Ponies* strapped to the front of his cart, in fact his cart looked brand new, but it was him. After what happened next, though, I almost wish I could say it wasn't.

"Moss Cart!" I said, running up to him. He turned my

way and looked at me, surprised. Maybe even a little bit scared.

"Moss Cart, hey! It's so good to see you." I was a little out of breath from excitement maybe, but I could tell he wasn't seeing me. Or he wasn't seeing someone he knew; he wasn't seeing Firefly. I have grown a little, and I was probably looking a little different from the Firefly he knew last summer, better fed and better dressed anyway.

"It's me, Moss Cart. Firefly!" He stopped and looked carefully at me then, shook his head.

"Sorry, girl. Who?" He looked puzzled and weirded out. I couldn't tell if he was high or not, but to be fair he hadn't seen me in months and I was out of context. We were meeting on a busy street, a long way from the park last summer.

Maybe he left the park anyway after the baseball-bat night, and forgot about me?

"It's okay, Moss Cart. It's Firefly. We were friends last summer." I tried not to let my voice get wobbly. He shook his head and shrugged.

"Sorry, Firefly. I don't remember things very well. You're good, though? Things okay?" he asked, and I suddenly had to blink back tears. Here was my friend, someone who helped me, someone I trusted. It was his voice, his same kind face and manner, and he didn't remember me.

I nodded. "Yeah, things are okay, Moss Cart. Look, I got something for you. Stay there. Don't move." I ran back to Aunt Gayle's car and grabbed the bag of clothes for Jennie's from the back seat.

"Everything okay?" Aunt Gayle asked, a little alarmed. Tears were running down my cheeks now.

"Yeah," I whimpered. "Just an old friend," I managed to get out in that strangled voice. Then I ran back and gave Moss Cart the bag. I shoved it into his hands.

"What's this?" he asked, rightly surprised. I took off my Aunt-Gayle-knitted hat and gloves too, and shoved them at him.

"Just a gift from your friend Firefly, Moss Cart," I said, and he smiled. He looked at something behind me, and I turned to see Aunt Gayle standing there with two bags of groceries.

I grabbed them and handed them to him, too.

He smiled that smile of his. "Thank you, ladies," he said gently. Then he looked at me and added, "Firefly," like he was introducing himself.

Then he really broke my heart.

He reached into his cart and pulled out … a soccer ball wrapped in a pink blanket. He pushed his beloved Baby at me, and I took her, cuddled her, said "Hello, Baby," then gave her back to him. He put Baby back among the clothes and groceries in his cart. He looked content, pleased that I shared his Baby with him.

"Thanks, Moss Cart," I said. Then he waved and pushed his cart along and away.

"Friend of yours?" Aunt Gayle asked as we walked back to the car. And I looked at her and nodded, then I burst into tears. Real, stormy, bubbling snot and sobbing tears. And my aunt, well, let's just say for the first time I accepted her big hug, and I didn't mind.

I didn't mind it at all.

I have a lot to thank Moss Cart for. He was the person who told me about Jennie's, and the free clothes, food, and counseling. He also told me not to worry about showing ID, just tell them I'm sixteen if they ask. And Moss Cart was also the first person to tell me that I was the kid, not the parent.

Now that I've found him once, I can find him again. It doesn't matter if he knows me or not, I know him. Aunt Gayle agreed right away; we'll find Moss Cart again, with more gifts of clothes and food, whenever I want.

Then the other not-so-okay thing is Joanne-the-mother.

A few days later, Aunt Gayle went to see her. When Aunt Gayle came back quiet, I asked how it went, and she just said, "hopeful, but also not really any different." I guess they'd argued about something, but Aunt Gayle really didn't want to talk about it and I respect that.

I know that loving Joanne is a lot of work.

I haven't been to see Joanne-the-mother, but she has written me more letters, which I read and it's fine. And

Charlie and I are working on writing one back to her. The therapist is helping, too. I mostly write one then tear it up which is why I haven't sent anything through Sharlene Baker yet, but maybe one day.

Maybe.

Whatever happens with Joanne, though, the fireflies will still be there in the park, safe, beautiful, flickering in the twilight for everyone.

And for me.

Acknowledgments

I've been lucky enough in my career to write stories about lost gargoyles, a flying girl, a monster of fog, a giant's hand, a doppelgänger, time travel at the fair, zombie pirates, robots, and more. With *Firefly*, I've written about a teenager living with her aunt in a costume shop, my first piece of realistic fiction.

Why did I wander from magic realism, fantasy, and dystopia with this book?

The answer is simple: I was inspired by a gifted family member and a fantastic setting. The character of Aunt Gayle is inspired by my sister-in-law, who was a spectacularly gifted costume designer, and who did in fact build a costume company with seven million pieces in it. I have her to thank for the kernel of this story too, since she once told me she had an idea for a flickering costume …

The only tribute I can offer her is this book, so I hope Aunt Gayle and her costume shop live long for you, dear reader.

I should add that only Aunt Gayle is inspired by a real person though; all the other characters in this story are fictional.

Every book travels a long road before publication of course, and there are many to thank …

Thanks to my wonderful publishing family at DCB Young Readers: Barry Jowett (who was quick to say yes), Sarah Jensen, and Sarah Cooper, for their continued faith in me. Many thanks too to Marc Côté, publisher of parent company Cormorant Books, for letting me do this thing. I've been incredibly lucky in such a talented, dedicated team. Thanks also to Sylvia McConnell, my first publisher, who got this book party started in 2009.

Many thanks to Julie McLaughlin, the illustrator of the beautiful covers of this book; she captured perfectly the feel of the story, the look of the Toronto shop, and Firefly too.

And no book can live without dedicated early readers and supporters. Thanks to Doris Montanera, Gillian Kerr, April Lindgren, Rebecca Upjohn, Monica Kulling, KB, and Peter Skilleter, who held the lamp high.

Thanks to my nephew (who now runs the costume shop) for cheering me on, for answering my many questions, and for giving his blessing to this book. And thanks to my children Sarah and Ben, who worked with their aunt, uncle, and cousin in the shop for many summers as teenagers, and who shared their stories about lobsters, carrots, medieval warriors, and more.

Finally thanks to Paul, who loved his sister, and this book.

This work of fiction is inspired by a family member, yes, but it's really about the love, friendship, and courage in every family. I hope in that way, it reminds you of yours.

Philippa Dowding, 2021

Philippa Dowding is an award-winning children's author, poet, musician, and copywriter based in Toronto.

As a copywriter, she has won industry awards for *Maclean's*, *Chatelaine*, *Today's Parent*, *Zoomer*, *Canada's History* and more. Her poetry and short fiction have been published in print and online journals across North America, including *The Adirondack Review*, *Taddle Creek*, *Middle Shelf* magazine, and *The Literary Review of Canada*.

Her multi-award-winning children's books include *The Lost Gargoyle* series, a *White Raven* selection by the International Youth Library in Munich; *The Nightflyer's Handbook* series; and the award-winning *Weird Stories Gone Wrong* series. The second book in that series, *Myles and the Monster Outside* (2015), won the OLA Silver Birch Express Honour Book award.

Her middle-grade dystopia, *Oculum* (2018), was nominated for the OLA Silver Birch Award and the SYRCA Diamond Willow Award, and has been optioned for television. *Firefly* (2021) is her thirteenth book for children.

Philippa has an M.A. in English Language and Literature from the University of Toronto, and she is also an accomplished guitarist and composer with several recorded works.

You can find more about Philippa, her writing, poetry, and music, at pdowding.com.

We acknowledge the sacred land on which Cormorant Books operates. It has been a site of human activity for 15,000 years. This land is the territory of the Huron-Wendat and Petun First Nations, the Seneca, and most recently, the Mississaugas of the Credit River. The territory was the subject of the Dish With One Spoon Wampum Belt Covenant, an agreement between the Iroquois Confederacy and Confederacy of the Ojibway and allied nations to peaceably share and steward the resources around the Great Lakes. Today, the meeting place of Toronto is still home to many Indigenous people from across Turtle Island. We are grateful to have the opportunity to work in the community, on this territory.

We are also mindful of broken covenants and the need to strive to make right with all our relations.